Peril at the Potluck

▪

Maile Spencer Honolulu Tour Guide Mysteries

▪

Kay Hadashi

Peril at the Potluck.
Maile Spencer Honolulu Tour Guide Mysteries.

Cover art by Kingwood Creations.
ISBN: 9798591092368

Table of Contents

Chapter One

Maile watched through the peephole in her door as her neighbors embraced and kissed goodbye before the husband left for work. Only a few hours before, she'd played a similar scene at the end of a date. It had been a happy scene, the kiss a thrill. But she had enough changes coming in her life; she didn't need to add romance to it.

Or did she?

Seeing her neighbor turn for her door, Maile opened hers hoping she'd have someone to chat with for a while.

"Rosamie, would you like some tea?"

Her young friend's face burst into a smile. They were the same age, but while Rosamie already had two kids and another on the way, Maile was nursing a broken heart and damaged life, and all she had to show for it were divorce papers.

"Is there coffee? Hubby won't let me have coffee because of the baby. He thinks it'll get hooked on the caffeine."

Maile let her in and went about the task of switching from a boiling kettle of water to making coffee, using the last of her grounds. "It's only been a few weeks. I don't think your baby can get addicted to caffeine yet." After making the brew, she took the two steaming mugs to her dinette table.

"How'd your date go last night?" Rosamie asked.

"I had a date?" Maile said, trying to hide her face by sipping from the mug.

"You were dressed pretty when a man brought you home late in the evening. That's a date."

Maile wasn't the only one in the building to peek out their peephole to spy on neighbors. "Oh, him. It was good, nice."

"Just nice?"

"Yeah, nice."

"How long have you known him? Rosamie asked.

"Brock? Since we were kids. But somewhere along the way, we just sort of lost touch with each other, different schools, different churches, you know how it goes. Then last year we met again. We have a few things to work out before going any further."

"From the looks of the kiss you gave him, the only thing the two of you need to work out is which side of the bed you'll wake up on in the morning."

Maile tore open several packets of sugar for her coffee and stirred it in. "Not in any kind of hurry, Rosamie. I can't be."

"Yes, you're thinking of going to the mainland. No reason you can't have some fun before then."

"I also don't want to leave town and take a baby with me. That's definitely not in the plan."

"You only live once, Maile."

"Maybe so, but I need to be wise with how I manage my life. I wasn't very smart about it the first time I got married. I still have some personal things I need to do before starting a family."

"Like?" Rosamie asked.

"See more of the world. Live in a couple of different places from here. Meet other people besides local Honolulu people. The only other people I've ever met were patients at the hospital and tour guests, and I never got to know them very well. It was odd, how they'd come here for a few days, have a grand time, and then go home again. I always wondered what their ordinary lives were like."

"You're coming back here once you're done exploring the world?"

"Eventually. And I'll tell you the same thing I tell my mother every time she gripes at me about it. When I get back, I can get a good job, find a nice guy to marry, and then start my family. And in that order. I'm still in my twenties, and everybody thinks I'm getting too old to see the world, that somehow I'm missing my chance at motherhood. I don't see the big hurry."

"Gonna start the family with that guy last night?" Rosamie asked. "He's that cop you know, right?"

"Brock?" Maile refilled their mugs. "If I'm leaving town, I can't ask him to come with me. He's working on becoming a detective, and I'm not asking him to set aside his career to follow me around the countryside. That's why I'm not going to pursue anything with him right now. But if he's still available when I come home, I'll give him a call."

"Giving him a call someday isn't very romantic, Maile."

"It might be the best I can do. We could write and call each other, I suppose."

"I hope you do. Maybe for once one of those long-distance relationships will work. If anybody can make it happen, you can, Maile."

“Nothing is carved in stone yet.” Maile changed the subject to what had been occupying her mind for weeks. “When do you guys move?”

“We’re paid up in this dump for the rest of the month. That gives us two more weeks. Hubby went out to look for boxes to pack our stuff. The sooner we can get out of here, the better, as far as I’m concerned. When would you leave?”

“Not till after New Year’s. I’ll stick it out here in Coconut Palms until the bitter end.”

“Don’t want to move in with your mother for a while?” Rosamie asked. “Or maybe with Brock?”

“I’m not moving in with a guy I still don’t know well.” Maile thought of the changes in her mother’s life right then. “Our church’s reverend and she are thinking of getting married soon. I don’t want to get in the way of their romance.”

“Maybe they already are married? Just haven’t said ‘I do’ or filled out the paperwork yet?”

For some reason, Maile didn’t blush over the personal question. “Kinda hard to think of my mom of having a husband again. My dad died when I was a little kid. It’s just been her, my brother, and me ever since. I wonder if it would feel crowded if we let someone else in our private little club?”

“Is he good to her?” Rosamie asked.

“He’s very sweet, the kindly reverend we deserve to have at church. When he gives Sunday School classes after church, he makes them fun by playing his ukulele while singing the lesson.”

Rosamie chuckled. “He plays a ukulele during class?”

"He's not terribly musical. His ukulele is as old as the hills, and he doesn't play any better than he sings, but it makes it fun for the kids."

"I'd love to go to church there, but my in-laws would freak out if we went anywhere but the place we got married."

"Hurry up if you do. Reverend Ka'uhane is going to retire soon, and needs to train his replacement. I guess the new minister will move into the Reverend's place when he moves in with my mom." Maile sighed. "More changes to look forward to."

They chatted about the small, Hawaiian congregation Maile attended in Manoa Valley, and how it was so different from the large Catholic church Rosamie's family went to.

"Running in the big race tomorrow, right?" Rosamie asked.

"Finally, it's here," Maile said. "I get the idea tomorrow it's going to be a busy day. All I want to do before then is sit around and rest, maybe stretch my legs with a walk, and get a big meal. I have errands to run instead. Any idea of what I can take to a potluck? Not like I can make anything decent in my kitchen."

"Want me to make something? How many people?"

"Probably fifty, and whatever homeless people show up for a free meal."

"Just buy some of those big jugs of soda. One of each kind." Rosamie nodded. "That's good enough. What's the potluck for?"

"I've told you about the Manoa House?"

"That club for Hawaiian people?"

"Right. Each December, we get someone new to run the place in the coming year. Thank goodness I'm done with it. After me running the place for a year, I'm surprised we still have a membership. The potluck is to elect a new person and to say goodbye to the out-going chump."

"If the potluck's for you, you don't have to take nothing. Hey! Maybe that Brock guy will be there?"

"I'm sure he will. In fact, I'm nominating him to run the organization in the coming year. He can't do any worse than I have."

"See? Now you have a reason to call him all the time while you're away, to see how things are going. You're smart, Maile!"

Maile chuckled. "I wish."

"Mrs. Taniguchi must be having a fit, with two renters moving out at the same time," Rosamie said.

"Not my problem," Maile said, taking their mugs to the sink to rinse. "I've gotta say, I'll miss you guys, maybe even Mrs. Taniguchi, but I'm not gonna miss this junky apartment."

"We'll miss you, too. Maybe you can come over sometime for dinner? I can make something special in my new kitchen. We could laugh and tell stories about what it was like to live here. When do you leave?"

"Still nothing carved in stone," Maile said while walking her neighbor to the door. She hated lying to her friend, as she already knew exactly when she'd leave Honolulu. "I'll let you know."

"Hey! Maybe you could bring you your boyfriend, Brock?"

"Not my boyfriend." Maile gave Rosamie a nudge in the back to get her out the door. "With the holidays here, and the marathon tomorrow, I'm too busy to even think about him."

Once her neighbor was gone, Maile's phone rang with a call from an unknown caller.

"You Spencer?" the man's gruff voice asked.

"Yes. Who's this?"

"Kennedy, from Honolulu A-1 Wreckers. You the one with a car to unload?"

"I almost forgot you were coming today. You're here already?"

"Right out front. Which one is it?" he asked.

"The old orange car around the corner. I'll be down in just a minute." She dressed in a hurry and went downstairs barefoot. Dressed in gray overalls that barely stretched across his potbelly, the tow truck driver already had his truck backed up to Maile's car, ready to hitch it. "I was told I'd get a hundred dollars for it."

"Who told you that?"

"Your boss, Manny."

"Manny's not here, is he?"

"Take your hitch off my car, then."

"Look, lady. You want to get rid of it or not?"

"I want to get rid of it, but I also want the hundred bucks I was promised on the phone by your boss." She got her phone from her pocket. "Want me to call him?"

"I got better things to do than stand here and argue with you. You want me to take it or you want to stand here and talk about it?"

"Stand here and talk about it, if that's what makes you happy. Look, I know how this works. You get a car from me, spend a few hours fixing a couple things with parts from your junkyard, then sell it for five hundred. That's why your boss offered me the hundred dollars cash that I know is in your pocket right now, money he gave you right before your drove here." Maile stuck out her hand. "Give me the hundred or I call your boss."

"How you know I'm not Manny?"

"Even junkyard bosses don't drive tow trucks. Anyway, you said your name is Kennedy before, and Manny's last name is Rodriguez."

After he stuffed a wad of cash in her hand, she handed over the title and key. Once they were both satisfied, he went back to work hitching up her car to the tow truck. Maile watched as he drove off, and noticed the simple one-fingered salute he gave her before rounding the turn.

Maile counted the twenties again before clenching them in her hand. "Hated to see it go, but they'll get a big surprise when they find out there's a lot more wrong with that thing than junky spark plugs."

Chapter Two

At the potluck that day, Maile wanted to conduct the Manoa House business as quickly as possible, before sneaking off to do the rest of her errands. She would be glad to hand over the reins of the club, but she also knew it would be the last time she'd see many of the members for a while. Few people knew she was leaving town soon, and none of them knew why or where she was going, a secret she was keeping close to her vest. As it was, they were holding the potluck at a canoe club just across the Ala Wai Canal from Waikiki. She wasn't sure why, but the annual meeting was normally held at the Manoa House, with a picnic-style barbecue in the back garden. For some reason, it had to be different this year.

Maile had a pile of laundry to wash, and only one clean outfit, something she wouldn't have worn as a tour guide. The long skirt and long-sleeved blouse were modest, almost dowdy, and the high collar didn't make it any sexier. It was not the impression she wanted to make on Brock that day. In spite of what she'd told Rosamie earlier, she really did want to turn Brock's head. If she worked it right, she might be able to finagle a ride from him, help with her errands, and have a meal together later.

When she left her little one-room apartment behind, she went to a nearby convenience store to buy the sodas. Filling a knapsack and two bags with bottles, she set off toward Waikiki. A bus took her most of the way, followed by a hurried crossing through a busy intersection and across a bridge. From over the broad

Ala Wai Canal, she had a view of the outrigger canoe club, a popular sport in Honolulu. While one canoe was just coming in from a workout, club members were setting up long tables for food in the shade of a large pavilion. A sizable group was there, and a couple of them were hanging a banner of some sort. Just as she predicted, a couple of homeless guys were already hanging around, chatting with folks arranging food bowls, hoping for handouts.

While that went on, another outrigger canoe that belonged to the club was paddled to shore. Maile watched intently as it was hauled out of the water by the paddlers. There was something about shirtless men and Polynesian tattoos…

By the time she got to the tables full of casseroles and salads, both homeless men had plates of food and were sitting in the shade having their meal. Maile poured cups of soda for them.

"You're not their waitress, Maile," Lopaka said. He had been the driver of the tour van when she still worked as a guide. Now that she was suddenly owner of the company, she wasn't sure what her role was. "They can come get their own drinks."

"I know. It just seems like someone needs to be nice to these guys."

"They're like cats. Feed them once and you can't get rid of them."

"So cynical," Maile said. She took the drinks over to the men, chatted for a moment, before rerunning to Lopaka, now making a plate of food of his own.

"What'd you talk to them about?" he asked.

"I told them this was a private party, but they could eat as much as they want, as long as they didn't become bothersome."

"You actually said bothersome?"

"What else was I supposed to say? They're not causing trouble, and we have plenty to eat already, and even more is coming. We can spare a few plates of food."

"You're too nice, Mai. You needed to get rid of them."

"I figure that as soon as they wander off, they'll tell all their friends free food is available at the park, and we'll be swarmed. The longer two of them sit there feeding themselves, the longer it is before two dozen others show up."

"Good idea. You've learned a few things since becoming a tour guide. I just wish you hadn't quit."

"Yeah, well, it was time. Not that I'm looking forward to running the company."

"You never have told me what your plans are. Everyone coming here today is expecting a big announcement."

"You'll have to wait, just like everyone else. Where're the wife and kids?" she asked.

"The kids are running loose in the ball fields in a giant game of tag. Betty is chatting with the gaggle of ladies around the corner. Just so you know, they have a surprise for you."

"For me?"

Lopaka nodded as he bit into a chicken leg. "Big farewell banner, and a gift card to that fancy department store on the mainland."

Maile watched as another outrigger came to shore, the half-dozen men carrying it to where it belonged. "I wish they hadn't done that. This is becoming a much bigger deal than necessary."

"Just go with it and act surprised. Their feelings would be hurt if you don't. Why are you dressed like a missionary?"

"The only clean clothes I had. I look like a missionary?"

"Maybe you could push the sleeves up and roll up the hem of the dress?"

"Yeah, that wouldn't look stupid at all." She waved air into her face with her hat.

"What's the deal with your hair?" he asked.

"What's wrong with it?"

"Kinda lumpy."

"I need to wear it in a braid for the marathon tomorrow and practiced making a French braid. Is it coming apart?"

Lopaka kept chewing. "Lopsided."

Maile put her hat back on and pushed it low to her ears. While they talked, her mother and Reverend Ka'uhane showed up, bringing her Aunt Kelani visiting from Maui with them. Kealoha had brought freshly pounded poi, one of Maile's favorites, and the Reverend was wearing his smile, something that always warmed her heart. He'd also brought his old ukulele to play. If she was going to have a stepfather, she couldn't have picked a better husband for her mother.

On their heels came Brock. When she first saw him getting out of his pickup truck, she couldn't help but smile, still thinking of the kiss they'd shared the night before. That had almost led to her inviting him in, and it had taken a lot of courage not to. She began walking to the parking lot to meet him, but stopped when he went around to the passenger side of the pickup. Opening it, a woman stepped out. If Maile looked frumpy, this woman was the opposite, in shorts and a tight blouse, glossy long hair fluttering in the wind, wedges on her feet to make her legs look longer. The waitress at a restaurant where local cops like to eat, her and Maile's paths had crossed in the past. The picture was complete when she took Brock's arm while he carried bags of food with his other hand.

"Miss Wong," she hissed. "There's not supposed to be anything between them, but they sure look cozy right now."

Another outrigger arrived and was lifted onto the bank by the paddlers. This time, it wasn't as much of a treat to watch the Polynesian men go through their efforts. Once the paddles were safely stowed, the men put on shirts and found something to eat at the potluck table, ending the show. What she couldn't figure out was why so many canoes were arriving then, and that she recognized very few of the paddlers. Most were heavily tattooed in Polynesian tribal decorations, something Maile had always been torn trying to decide if she liked so many tattoos.

When the group thought everyone had shown up for what she figured would be her last meeting as the ad hoc leader of the Manoa House, she found a place at the front. With one last glance at Miss Wong, she got started.

"As all of you know, my tenure is coming to an end soon, and we'll need someone who can watch over finances and conduct meetings."

"Why don't you do it for another year?" someone asked.

"Yeah! Just take it over permanent-like!"

"Well, you see, I've been exploring some opportunities to go out of town for a while."

"Where you goin'? Work on Maui?"

"Big Island?"

"Probably to the mainland. But that's not why we're here today. I'd like to nominate Brock Turner to take my place as Manoa House President. He knows the needs of our community, has the time…" Maile looked at Brock, Miss Wong right next to him, thought of her kiss with him the night before, and forced a smile. "…and certainly has the energy for it."

There was a near-unanimous vote for Brock, the only holdout being Lopaka, who voted for Maile to remain in the position, and in Honolulu, 'where she belonged'. She went through the little bit of business there was to discuss, scholarship money renewal to local college kids, a work party to paint the Manoa House, and a search for a volunteer to maintain the house landscaping. With a sense of poignancy, and while the two homeless guys looked on from a picnic table, Maile announced the meeting was done.

"We're not done quite yet, Maile," Lei-lei said. She was one of Maile's oldest friends, someone she'd gone to nursing school with, and a hospital workmate. Maile watched as the canoers stood and removed their shirts again, almost two dozen of them. They went out to a level area in the sun and lined up in rows and columns.

"What's going on?" Maile asked, even though she knew what was coming.

"There's no way we can let one of our beloved sisters leave her job as our leader without a haka as a send-off!" Lei-lei said. She nodded to the men, who got the haka ceremonial dance started.

Maile watched while the traditional dance was performed in her honor, the men chanting loudly, stomping the ground, and lifting arms skyward in unison. Even though it was Maori in origin, the act had spread across many of the Polynesian cultures, and was often performed at sporting events in Hawaii. After the two-minute performance, the men wrapped it up by climbing into their canoes and paddling off again.

That's when Maile noticed her eyes were wet, and that all the potluck attendees were looking at her. All she wanted to do then was leave. She'd had plans to spend some of the afternoon with Brock, or at least do some overt flirting, but that was gone now that Miss Wong was by his side.

Keeping her from rushing off was Reverend Ka'uhane going to a chair toward the front of the group, taking his ukulele with him. Coming from the restroom to join him were Lei-lei and Sandra, another old friend. They had hurriedly dressed in hula clothes while the haka was being performed, and once the Reverend began to strum, they began a dance. It was a hula Maile knew well, one that carried a heavy farewell message. Realizing it was being performed for her, a few tears ran down. She wondered if they knew more about her plans than she'd let on. So far, only Lopaka knew the details of what she was considering doing, and only after she'd let it accidently slip one day.

Once the hula was done, and Reverend Ka'uhane's singing and strumming thankfully ended, the ukulele was set aside and Maile was given a few hugs and well wishes. She knew she needed to make one last pass through everyone to say goodbye, and as she did, she deftly sidestepped Brock, who was aiming straight for her. With a glance, she saw Miss Wong at the food table, picking through what was left. When he continued toward her, Maile ducked into the ladies' restroom.

"Can't sit in here for the rest of the day," she mumbled, waving air into her face with her hat. Thinking of what Lopaka had said earlier, she tried tucking in lumps and bumps of her braid. By the time she left the restroom, a few of her friends were getting ready to leave. That seemed like a great idea, to walk someone to their car and then keep going, hoping to leave without a scene between her, Brock, and Miss Wong. Right then, she wanted to let him have it across the chops, which wasn't much of a farewell gesture.

Miss Wong was still at the table of food, loading what must've been a second plate of food, Brock at her side. When he noticed Maile exit the restroom, he came over to her, smiling.

"You don't want to deal with me right now, Turner. Oh, excuse me, Sergeant Turner."

"What's wrong?" he asked, acting innocent.

She looked past him and nodded her head in Miss Wong's direction.

"You don't understand," he said.

"All I need to understand about her are what I see with two eyes and a jealous heart." Maile noticed what Miss Wong was eating. "Hitting that shrimp pretty hard for someone who came to a potluck empty handed."

Once they were done leveling frowns at each other, Brock collected his date and led her away from the food table. When Maile's vision focused again, she noticed Reverend Ka'uhane at the table looking for something to put on his plate. Still a little hungry herself, she joined him there.

"Thanks for the song, Reverend. Truly a blessing to have you sing for me."

"Your mother suggested it. She enjoys my singing, but just between you and me, the kids make fun sometimes, don't they?"

"They love you for the fun lessons you give. We all do."

"You're very diplomatic, Maile."

She watched as he loaded his plate. "That shrimp has been out of the refrigerator for quite a while, Reverend."

"Should be good for bait."

"Oh, you like to fish? I never knew that."

"More like feeding the fish. Nice day for a potluck at the park. Who's the tall lady with the kids you were talking to earlier?"

"Mayor Kato, from Maui. She's a physician and has come to volunteer for the medical tent in tomorrow's marathon. I asked her to come to the potluck. I was hoping to ask her a few questions about something."

"She's a runner?"

"I think she surfs. Maybe I can get some inspiration from her about my ideas for going to the mainland."

He switched languages to Hawaiian when someone else came to the table. "It would be sad to see you go, Hoku."

"For me, too. Honolulu has always been my home, but I'd miss my mother the most."

"Of course you would. She doesn't understand why you're being so secretive about your plans."

"I'll tell her soon enough." Maile took the last of the poi to eat. "I can't believe I'd be so far away from her. She's always been just across town. Soon...I don't know."

"Her friends will still be here. She's stronger than what you realize."

Maile stacked a few empty plates. "Stronger than I am."

"Your aunt is thinking of coming back to Oahu. I was just talking with her a few minutes ago. I think she misses Honolulu more than what she realizes."

"It sounds like she has so many friends on Maui already."

"None of them are male companions. I think that's what she aches for," the Reverend said.

"No shortage of middle-aged men on either island."

The minister she'd known all her life, the man that kept their small congregation together through thick and thin, wandered off to find Maile's mother, Kealoha. A suntanned hand pointed to something in a serving bowl in front of Maile.

"Mind if I have some of that?"

Maile handed over the bowl. "Sure."

"Thanks."

The voice was familiar. Maile got a surprise when she looked at the girl. "Oh, hello, Suzie…Susan."

"My dad said you invited me. I guess it's okay I'm here."

"Of course, it's okay." Maile shook the young woman's hand. Every other time they'd made physical contact, it had been during fights in the police station cellblock. "I'm glad you came. Be careful with the shrimp. It's been out for a while."

"I don't eat it anyway. I'm…my mom raised me to be vegetarian."

"There're plenty of other things to eat here." Maile looked the girl up and down for a moment. That's all she really was, still a teenager that had made a few bad choices in life. That day, maybe because her father had told her to, her clothing was a little more subdued than the usual outfits she wore to walk the streets in Chinatown. "You look nice today. Cute outfit."

"Thanks. You look…"

"Like a missionary?"

"Like a school teacher."

They both chuckled over their personal inside joke.

"Not wearing your wig?" Maile asked.

"That thing was a pain in the neck. Mine's long enough to comb now. I might dye it blond or something."

"That'd be fun." Not knowing what to do with Susan, she sent her away to mingle with others. Oddly, she made a beeline to one of the other Japanese Americans there, that of Maui's mayor and her daughter, Therese. Wondering what she and the ten-year-old girl were talking about, Maile went close enough to eavesdrop. The conversation was in Japanese, and Maile was surprised that both of them seemed so well versed in it. After a few more minutes, Susan came back to Maile.

"I see you met Doctor Kato. She's the mayor over on Maui."

"Everybody knows her. I heard she might run for governor next year."

"I hope so. Nobody likes the one we have right now. You're good at Japanese," Maile said.

"My mother was raising me to be a good Japanese girl, with language and religion. What she never knew was that I found johns…" Susan smiled in an apologetic way. "…foreign customers in Chinatown using Japanese."

There was no avoiding the million-dollar question. "What are you doing for work?"

Susan acted defensive. "I don't do that stuff anymore. That's not why I'm here."

"I know. That's not why I asked."

"Why, then?" Susan said.

"I don't work as one anymore, but Manoa Tours needs a tour guide. Is that something you'd be interested in trying?"

Susan pointed at herself. "Me? A tour guide?"

"It's not such a bad job and the money is pretty good." Maile explained how she had recently become the owner of the company and had plans to grow it. "You could work with Lopaka, my old driver."

Maile called Lopaka over and explained her idea to him. He hesitated until she prodded him into the idea with a hint of a bonus. Lopaka put Susan through a job interview of his own while Maile continued to tidy the table of food. When he gave her the high sign, it was a done deal to Maile, that Susan was as good as hired. If he was willing to work with the girl, it was okay with her.

"Why're you and your friends being so nice to me?" Susan asked, helping Maile and another lady clean up the food table.

"Because you're being nice to us."

"Yeah, but what do you want from me in return?"

"Nothing."

"No strings attached?" Susan asked.

"Nope."

"Look, School Teacher…Maile. There're always strings attached."

"Maybe just this once there aren't. If you want that job, come to the Manoa Tours office Monday morning at eight o'clock."

"Dressed like a school teacher?"

"More like a tour guide. At least not dressed in your old clothes. Maybe your dad can take you shopping." Maile smiled at her new employee. She knew exactly what to do with a gift card for a fancy department store she'd received earlier. "Here. Use this to start a wardrobe for your new job."

"You're sure? That's a fancy place."

"Think of it as a hiring incentive bonus. I thought your dad was supposed to be here today?"

"He had some big police thing to do this afternoon." Susan nodded her head toward the parking lot. "Here he comes now."

Maile looked to see Detective Ota, a friend from the Honolulu Police Department and Susan's recently reunited father, walking from where he'd parked his sedan at an angle in the handicapped spaces. Another police car was there, and two uniformed cops were walking with him, aiming straight for the party.

"I wonder where they're going?" Maile muttered.

"Not here for me," Susan said, munching on a carrot stick while clearing away empty bowls. "That's all I care about."

"Me, too." Maile wondered if she should bring up a sensitive topic. "There's something I've always been curious about. Kinda personal."

"Why I left home so young?" Susan asked.

"Well, that. But did your dad ever arrest you?"

Susan's nerves must've cracked with the question because she dropped a casserole. "Sorry."

"I shouldn't have asked."

"No, it's alright. He never put the cuffs on me or read me my rights, if that's what you're wondering."

"He always has somebody else do that dirty work for him, huh?" Maile said.

A shy smile crept across Susan's face. "You too?"

Maile nodded. "He's kind of a softy with women."

"Totally. He'll pound the dickens out of some guy, but he's always kind to hoo…my old workmates."

Ota seemed to notice Maile and Susan watching him and the uniformed officer with him, but instead of coming their way, he angled off toward the canal. She looked in the direction the police were headed, and it was toward Brock, where he was talking with Miss Wong near an outrigger canoe. She had a hand on his chest in a flirtatious way, much the same as Maile had done the night before. Every muscle in Maile's body tightened as she continued to watch them have their moment in the sun.

"You like that guy, huh?" Susan asked.

"What guy?"

"You know what guy. Turner."

"Maybe once upon a time."

"Not anymore?"

"Not so much right now," Maile said.

"I wouldn't either if I caught him talking to her."

They watched as Detective Ota and the cop approached Brock and Miss Wong, who now had her hands on his hips.

"If I were you, I'd go slap the makeup off her face," Susan said. "But at least she's pretty."

"What's that supposed to mean?"

"Every hooker in Chinatown…all my old workmates…whatever. Everybody likes that guy."

Maile looked at her companion. "Oh?"

"Never got mean, never pushed us around, never cranked the cuffs down too tight. Half the time I was able to slip my hand out of the cuffs he put on me."

"Yeah, same with me, whenever they took me in."

"Not like you're a lot of trouble, School Teacher…Boss."

Maile had a quick fantasy of putting handcuffs on Miss Wong and throwing her into the canal only a few steps away. Ota and the two cops arrived at where Brock and Miss Wong were standing. The nature of their conversation changed from overtly friendly to one of surprise. When Miss Wong shook her head and took a step back, she bumped into the officer behind her. Ota was speaking then, and nodded to that officer. He then took over, trying to put handcuffs on Miss Wong as he spoke.

"No!" shouted a softly feminine voice. Whatever was going on, Miss Wong was refusing to be cooperative. Maile watched as the Chinese restaurant waitress looked at all four police officers surrounding her, still not allowing her hands to be cuffed. She settled her attention on Brock, shouted something in Chinese, and swung her leg up to kick him in the crotch. He was able to sidestep most of the kick.

"Wow, she's pissed about something," Susan said.

"Do you know her?" Maile asked.

"You mean does she work the streets? Not that I've ever seen."

They watched while there was a takedown of Miss Wong by Brock and another officer. In only seconds, her wrists were cuffed behind her back. Miss Wong was crying by then, the seam at the back of her shorts split open, her glossy hair going in every direction. When they helped her up to a standing position, she still resisted until she had no choice but to go to a waiting squad car. Maile watched as the woman was pushed into the back seat of the car and whisked away, with Brock following them in his pickup truck. While all that went on, Ota had been taking notes on his little notepad, and the small crowd of Maile's friends had watched intently.

"Off to the women's cellblock," Susan said. "She won't last long in there."

"Why not?"

"She's not tough."

"Either was I," Maile said.

"Are you kiddin' me? You were the toughest one I ever met in there."

"I guess I should take that as a compliment. But let's not spread it around that either one of us have been in jail, okay?"

When Susan went to mingle again, this time chatting with a pair of young men, Maile watched as Detective Ota walked to her.

"What happened with Miss Wong?" Maile asked right off.

"Under arrest for money laundering, for starts. I'm sure there'll be more charges once I piece together everything."

"Did you really have to arrest her here at our potluck?"

"That part was unfortunate. We've had a sting going on her and a few others, which involved a stakeout of the restaurant last night. I needed Turner to keep Wong away from the place to do that."

"Oh." That confirmed Maile's suspicions, that Brock had something, or someone, better to do all night than come into her room at the end of their date the evening before. "They spent the night together?"

"I don't know where he had her cooped up. I just needed Wong away from the restaurant while my undercover officer did her investigation. You know her as Lefty Louie."

"I forgot all about her. Anyway, I don't care about them."

"You've been talking with my daughter," he said, looking more at Susan than at Maile. "It even looked peaceful."

"Turning over a new leaf with each other. She's a likeable kid."

They both watched as the two young men wrote something on slips of paper and handed them over to Susan. "Sometimes a little too likeable. What did the two of you talk about?" he asked.

"Mostly about the job I offered her."

"Job?"

"She's my newest guide at Manoa Tours. Starts Monday."

"My daughter is going to work for you?" Ota asked.

"Hey, you're the one who wants her to turn over a new leaf. What better way than having to show some responsibility to someone other than herself? And a job is perfect for that."

"Is this a pity job, or do you really need someone?"

"A little of both. I can't give tours because I'll be busy learning the business side of tourism. Her Japanese sounds good, and I have a tour of Japanese housewives Monday afternoon."

"She knows that?" Ota asked, still with a tone of disbelief to his voice.

"She knows it, and promised to study the places they'll go on the tour. Even Lopaka has agreed."

"He'll watch over her as well as anyone else. Is there anything else that needs to be done?"

"I think she's waiting for you to take her clothes shopping at the mall. Do you mind?"

He shrugged. “Never done that with her before. What stores?”

“She knows which ones. Hey, you never have told me what there is between you and Lopaka.”

“Ask him.”

“That’s what he always says.”

Chapter Three

Most of the guests were gone by then. Once Ota collected his daughter and they left, Maile decided she'd had enough of the potluck. She went back to the covered pavilion to have one last cup of soda before leaving. She found her mother there looking worried while she watched Reverend Ka'uhane.

"What's wrong?"

"He lost his ukulele," her mother said, still watching.

Maile watched as several volunteers searched under tables and in trashcans. "When did he have it last?"

"He doesn't remember. The last time he remembers having it was when he played and sang. The old fool doesn't remember when or where he put it down."

"Don't call him that. Did he take it back to the car?"

Kealoha shook her head. "He checked there first."

Maile tried to remember if he had it with him when he got a plate of food. She went to the area where he'd sat while playing the ukulele earlier and searched. "It's got to be here in the pavilion. This is where he played it."

Several of the search party gathered to support the Reverend, who looked close to tears. He was told that all the trash bins had been searched carefully, as had the pavilion and picnic tables.

"Not in the canoes, either," someone said.

That's when Maile noticed a couple of the canoes had already departed, their muscular crews returning to their homeports. "Did anybody else play it?" she asked.

Blank faces looked back at her, everyone shaking their heads.

Maile put her hands on her hips and searched their faces again. "Nobody's playing a prank on Reverend Ka'uhane? Because it's not funny."

She watched as the kids were rounded up and interrogated. They all shook their heads, too.

"We no more steal Uncle Ka's ukulele," one boy said.

"We like his singing," a little girl whispered.

"Yeah, fun kind way of telling gospel stories."

"Well, the police just left," Maile said. "I should call someone to take a report."

"That's not necessary," the Reverend said. "It's just a simple old thing. No need for so much fuss."

"There needs to be a fuss," Maile said, while dialing Detective Ota's number. When he answered, it sounded noisy in the background, with several people shouting. "Am I interrupting something? Do you have a minute to take an official police business call?"

"Right in the middle of some chaos. Can it wait?"

"I guess."

With that, the line went dead. She wasn't sure if she should wait at the park for him to call her back, or leave. As it was, Reverend Ka'uhane was helping Kealoha into his car for the ride home. While others started to wander off with their half-eaten casseroles and empty salad trays, Maile continued to poke around dark corners in search of the missing musical instrument.

"Hello," someone said. The man's voice was familiar, but she couldn't place it. When she looked at him, she was surprised. A man and woman stood with canes in their hands.

"Brian! How are you?"

"You're Maile, right? This is your party?"

"Not really my party, but yes, this is the right place. How'd you know to come here?"

"Brock mentioned it. Is he still here?"

"No, he had somewhere to go a little while ago." Maile looked at the woman with him, obviously blind, with sunglasses and a white cane in her hand, her face turned slightly to one side instead of looking directly at Maile. "Who's your friend?"

"This is Amelia. She wanted to meet you. That's why we're here today."

Maile found the woman's hand and shook it. She was slender and they had similar physiques. "Me? I don't give tours anymore, Brian. If you guys call the Manoa Tours office, they can set you up with something that might be fun. I know Brock has the number."

"It's not for a tour," Amelia said. "I'd like to talk to you about the marathon tomorrow."

"Well, it starts at five in the morning so most runners will be done before the day gets hot. I think most people will get there an hour before then. Actually, the race goes right near here. I think the closest place it comes to Brock and Brian's apartment is at Kahala Mall. It should be pretty easy for you to walk there to watch…sorry, not to watch, but be a part of the scene. I bet the first runners should be going through there at around six or six-thirty."

"Amelia wants to run in it," Brian said.

"Oh?"

"I already have my race ticket. I had a guide, but she sprained her ankle on a training run yesterday. Then Brock mentioned you're running in it, and suggested I come talk to you about being my guide," Amelia said.

Brian excused himself to get a plate of food, with the help of a lady busy putting things away.

"I'm sorry, there might be some confusion. I used to be a tour guide, not a runner's guide. I don't know anything about that."

"But you're a trained competitive runner?" Amelia asked.

"Well, yes, in high school and college, but that was a few years ago. I've never done a marathon before. Just a couple of half marathons."

"What do you expect your time to be?"

"Better than five hours, and I'm hoping for something around four and a half."

"That's good, especially for a first marathon. I'm still hoping to break three."

"Hours? I can't run that fast. I couldn't keep up that pace even for a half marathon," Maile said. Deep down inside, that was her 'someday' quest, to run a three-hour marathon, something few runners ever accomplish.

Amelia continued to stand very still and straight-faced, a tough read for Maile to guess what she might've been thinking. "I just want to run tomorrow, mostly to keep my sponsors happy. I hardly care what our time would be. How would you deal with a leash?"

"I've seen vision-impaired runners with guides and their leashes. I guess as long as we both run the same speed, it should work out."

"It's more complicated than that. We'd need to match strides and arm swings. If a guide and blind runner get out of sync, it throws everything off. You'd also need to prompt me for turns and obstacles."

"Like how many feet away before we come to something?"

"Number of steps. What's your stride length at five miles?" Amelia asked.

That stumped Maile. Amelia was turning out to be much more scientific in her approach to running than she was. "I have no idea. The end of my half marathon is only half a mile per hour slower than mile five, if that helps any?"

"We can figure it out in the morning. That's assuming you'd like to run with me tomorrow?"

How could Maile say no? She had the chance to run with someone that needed her help, and the tradeoff would be that she might actually run a faster time than she had planned.

"Sure. Maybe I should call you later this evening so we can talk a little more about the details?"

Amelia's face brightened at the news. "We could do a training run today, if that's okay?"

"I, well, I know it sounds like I'm blowing you off, but I have a ton of things to do today, and this is supposed to be a rest day for tomorrow."

"Good idea. Maybe you can figure out your expected times and stride lengths at five mile increments before tomorrow morning?" Brian was just returning then, with a business card in his hand. "Honey, Maile's agreed to run with me tomorrow."

When Amelia called Brian 'honey', that answered that question for Maile.

"That's great!" He showed the business card to Maile. "I got this from one of your friends. Her name is Marsha Nakamoto. She said she knows you."

Maile read the card from the young ophthalmologist, a doctor that specializes in eyes. She had a clinic near Honolulu Medical Center where Maile used to work. "Yes, we knew each other in high school. She must've just finished her training. Are you looking for a new eye doctor?"

"She said she can get me into her clinic for an exam on Monday. She already made the appointment for me."

"I remember you told me it might still be months or even years before they could help you at the VA. You must realize that ophthalmologists are very expensive."

"Like you said, she's new and is trying to build a base. She offered me a discount because you guys are old friends. Do you know if she's any good?"

"She would do most of her work either in her clinic or in the operating room. I worked in the emergency room, a place eye docs try to avoid. I might be able to call around, though."

Brian pressed his forehead against Amelia's head. "See? I told you Maile would be able to help."

"She's doing a lot for us, Brian."

Maile chuckled. "Don't either of you get your hopes up too high. Amelia and I still need to run our race tomorrow, and without me tripping her too many times. And Brian needs some good news at his appointment."

Brian and Amelia whispered to each other like old lovers and kissed. Amelia's hand came up to touch his face. "Hey, behave yourself. I think she's still here."

"I was just going. Can you guys get to the bus stop okay?"

"We're good at finding things," Amelia said. "It might not be what we're looking for, but we always find something."

Tired and running late, Maile needed to hurry if she were to get her errands accomplished for the day. That meant a trip downtown with a visit that lasted barely an hour. It was an important one, the last step in her secret move to the mainland after the first of the year. When she was done with it, she was glad for the relief it brought to have the decision out of the way.

Walking to a bus stop, her phone rang with a call from Detective Ota. With everything else, she'd forgotten about the missing ukulele.

"What was happening before?" she asked him. "It sounded like a mess in the background of the call."

"Your friend, Miss Wong, happened."

"Not my friend."

"Whoever she is, that…she's feisty. It took four of us to get her into the cellblock. That's when things really got out of hand."

"Why?" Maile asked.

"It seems the ladies that work Chinatown are familiar with the Wong family, and decided to take out a little aggression on her. She fought back, though. By the time we had her back out of the cell, she'd already handed out two black eyes, knocked out a tooth, and enough hair had been pulled out of heads to weave a mullet."

Maile laughed. "For once, I wish I'd been there to see it!"

"What's your official police business?" he asked.

"I'm not sure if you met him at the potluck today, but Reverend Ka'uhane's ukulele went missing. We looked everywhere. Nothing."

"And you think it was stolen? Did you call police to make a report?"

"I called you."

"As much as I appreciate your faith in me as a detective, you need to call a police officer to make out a report. Then that gets sorted by importance, and is sent to someone's desk for investigation. And I'll tell you right now that unless it was exceptionally valuable and worth a lot of money, the time my department will spend on the case is minimal."

"That's what I figured. It's just an old thing. I doubt it's worth much."

"It would be easier for everyone if he were to buy a new one. Maybe it could be a Christmas gift from the congregation?"

"Barely have the money to pay the light bill each month." Maile tried to not let the disappointment ruin her day off. "Would it hurt the feelings of the police department if I looked into it?"

"It would hurt my feelings personally if you were hurt snooping around things and places that you shouldn't."

"I was thinking of going to pawnshops and music stores, to see if someone might've brought it in."

"Good idea, but wait a couple of days. It usually takes a while for something to show up on shelves. You could also look at online sales sites. You have a picture of the thing?"

"I have one of him playing it today. I'll send it in just a minute. How'd you know he's our congregation's minister?"

"I met your Aunt Kelani at the potluck today. She mentioned it."

"When did you meet her? You weren't there long enough."

"You were talking to Susan while glaring at Miss Wong, the current cellblock bi…never mind. She's a nice lady."

"Aunt Kelani? Don't get your hopes up, Detective. She lives on Maui and you don't."

With that, she sent the image from her phone to his, hoping something would come of it. When she got back to her place, there was no avoiding the mound of laundry that was waiting for her. It would take all evening to wash it at her mother's little cottage, so she packed it all in pillowcases and hiked it to the neighborhood laundromat.

Once she had three loads of wash going in adjacent machines, she grabbed a leftover magazine and sat in a chair, flipping from one page to another. The only clothes she had to wear that were clean were what she was planning to wear the next day for the run. Barely a few pages into the magazine and her phone rang with a call from Amelia. They talked about the role of a guide, and how best to deal with the two-foot leash that linked their wrists. Amelia talked about how fast she liked to run, and tried her best to keep an even pace and stride throughout. To marathon novice Maile, it all sounded very doable, and by the time she was folding her dry clothes, she was convinced they would do well in one of America's premiere marathon races.

"Well, it looks like I'm running a sub-four hour marathon tomorrow, whether I want to or not. I just hope I don't screw it up too much."

A cool mist started during her walk home from the laundromat, maybe a good omen for the weather the next day. In less than twelve hours, she needed to be at the start line near Ala Moana Mall. With any luck, the temperature would be cool for most of the race. What she did need to do was more carbo-loading to pack sugar into her muscles. She stopped in at the convenience store on the corner of her block for two packages of mini-doughnuts and milk.

"Two packages tonight," the clerk said. "You're getting out of control, Miss."

Maile grinned at his joke. "Maybe so. This time, one package is for breakfast." She grabbed a bottle of mango juice to go with it.

"You look too skinny to be a breakfast eater."

"I'll take that as a compliment." She told him about running in the next day's race, and how she'd been spending the last few weeks whittling every spare pound of fat from her body. "But that diet goes flying out the window as soon as I cross the finish line!"

When she went down her hallway, she tried her best to avoid the three creaks in the floorboards, hoping not to announce her arrival home. A new tenant had moved onto her floor recently, a young woman who used the room she rented more as a workspace than for living. The bed in Happenstance's room was used more than anything else, including the shower. As it was, Happenstance had taken a liking to Maile, wanting to spend her spare time with her discussing the 'business', and how much Maile could make if she joined forces with Happenstance. In recent days, that was all the incentive Maile needed to go on extra training runs, just to avoid those little meetings with the building hooker.

She got past that apartment successfully, only to meet Rosamie on her way out to a nearby park with the kids to run off some energy.

"Hey, can we talk?" Rosamie asked.

"Too tired to go to the playground. Maybe later in my place?"

"In an hour, okay?"

"Yeah, actually, I have a favor to ask you then."

"Sure, anything!" Rosamie said, as she was being pulled down the hall by her kids.

By the time her friend and the kids were back from the playground, Maile was out from her shower and had eaten a packet of doughnuts. She was also drinking copious amounts of water to make sure her body was completely hydrated for the next day's marathon run. By the time she and Amelia would be finishing the race, the temperature would be well into the seventies, maybe even tickling the eighty degree mark, much too hot to run so far. Five minutes after she heard the Mendoza kids clamor down the hall to their little apartment, there was a knock on her door. She let in Rosamie, who kept the door open. Maile saw across the way, that their door was propped open, also.

"The kids are still wound up, but I'm too tired to chase after them at the park. Every week, their energy seems to double," Rosamie explained. "You had a favor to ask?"

"It might be time consuming. What did you want to talk to me about?"

The ordinarily cheerful Rosamie had a hard time finding a cheerful smile. It went beyond that, with her face looking sad about something. "Just about moving."

"Oh, yeah, that." Maile sensed a long, heartfelt chat was coming. She tried smiling. "Having second thoughts about moving away from all this luxury and bliss at the Coconut Palms?"

"This old dump needs a can of gasoline and a match. But we've raised the kids here so far, and have our friends. You know what? This is going to take me a while to get out of my system. Maybe you should tell me your favor? You need a ride to the marathon in the morning?"

"I have a ride arranged, and it starts before you guys get up. What I need is for my hair to be French braided for tomorrow, and I can't do a decent job of it myself. You know how to make it so it's tight and not bouncing around?"

Rosamie finally smiled. "I'm the expert! I do that for my daughter all the time. You want one big a down the middle, or one on each side?"

"One on each side that meet in the middle in the back. That's what a teammate did for me when i used to compete." She bit her lip, concerned about something. "The thing is, you need to keep quiet you did this."

Rosamie patted Maile's hand. "It's okay. I really am good it this."

"No, I mean this is sort of a big deal."

"Super big deal running in the marathon tomorrow! Whatever I can do to help!"

"I appreciate that." Maile couldn't figure out how to explain, and it was too late to find someone else, so she pulled out her dinette chair and had a seat, handing over her comb and rubber bands. "While you do that, you can tell me about moving."

Rosamie went to work on hair that had already been combed out and parted. "I never knew your hair was so long."

"I usually keep it bundled up. Otherwise, the wind blows it all over."

"It's so long. Maybe I should cut some of this off?"

"Huh?"

"It would take me five minutes. I'm good at it, really! Real professional."

"I'm sure you'd do great, but maybe you don't understand about Hawaiians and their hair."

"Always so wavy. I wish mine was like yours," Rosamie said.

"It sure is. We also have some beliefs, something other people might call superstitions. We believe our mana is reflected in our hair. You know what mana is?"

"Like your internal power, right?"

"Some people might call it our essence, or divine personal strength. It's as important to us as hula or prayer. I guess it's one of the few things leftover from our old kapu system of cultural norms and laws, that a woman must have long hair to perform the hula."

Rosamie began braiding along one side. "You still do hula? I'd love to see the Merrie Monarch sometime."

"I haven't been in that since I was a kid. But if I did something to my hair, my mother would freak. Even allowing a non-Hawaiian to touch it could be troublesome."

"I just go to the salon occasionally and let them deal with it," Rosamie said. "I have their business card at home. I'll give it to you later. Maybe you can do something and your mom wouldn't notice?"

"She'd notice if even one hair was missing. In fact, she's the only one to ever have cut my hair." Getting a thought, Maile got her phone and found the calendar. "Akua moon on the first of the month."

"Nice way to start the New Year, with a full moon."

"Yep. Perfect." Maile put away her phone, needing to change the subject. "I saw your hubby bring home moving boxes earlier. Already packing up?"

"We're moving earlier than planned. We want to be in our new place before Christmas so we can decorate a tree and open presents there. We've never had a real tree to decorate. The kids are excited about that. We don't even have ornaments."

"That'll be fun for them."

"Gonna miss you, Maile. You have to drop by for a while."

"Maybe on Christmas Eve. My mom would kill me if I didn't spend Christmas day with her and Kenny. I suppose our congregation minister will be there, too."

When Rosamie finished braiding one side, she had Maile hold onto it while she worked on the other side.

"You still haven't told me where you're gonna work, or even where you're going on the mainland."

"Still not definite, but I should know pretty soon. If I know by then, I'll tell you on Christmas Eve." After telling the lie, she needed to change the subject. "I already know what I want to bring the kids for a gift, something they can use together."

"You don't have to bring them anything. The new place isn't all that big."

"Actually, it's perfect for Christmas and something all of you will enjoy."

Rosamie once again moaned and groaned about having to move, but Maile knew deep down inside, Rosamie was looking forward to getting out of their tiny apartment and into a nice neighborhood. "At least I won't have to explain to the kids about Happenstance anymore."

"You mean why she has so many friends showing up all the time?" Maile asked. She handed over the first braid so Rosamie could start weaving them together in back.

"And her clothes."

"You'd think she could take a shower occasionally."

Rosamie stalled in her work. "Not much of an advertisement for her services, huh?"

Maile laughed. "Maybe that's why the guys don't stick around for long?"

"Crazy what some people will do for money. It almost seems easier to get a real job than do what she does."

Maile winced against the tugging and pulling, wondering how much of her hair was being pulled loose. "Are you almost done?"

"Just putting the last of the rubber bands on. You'll have to sleep with a shower cap on your head if you want this to look pretty in the morning."

Maile looked in her bathroom mirror. Rosamie had worked something of a minor miracle in getting the complex hairdo smooth and flat to her head. "By the time we're halfway through the race, my running partner and I won't care a whit what we look like. We'll just be looking for the finish line."

Figuring a few photos would be taken of her and Amelia in the morning, and simply wanting to look her best at least at the start line, Maile took Rosamie's suggestion and wore a shower cap when she went to bed. Just as she was turning off her little lamp, her phone rang.

"I need to learn to turn this thing off," she muttered, grabbing it from the nightstand. She recognized the number and wasn't sure if she wanted to answer. Maybe it was good news. "Detective Ota, did you find Reverend Ka'uhane's ukulele?"

"Not yet. I thought you were going to look into that for me?"

"Not till the day after tomorrow," she said. "I'm a little busy tomorrow."

"Big race tomorrow, right?"

"We start running promptly at five AM, yes. And the sooner the world turns itself off tonight, the sooner I get to sleep. Once again, may I help you with something?"

"Sorry. I didn't notice how late it was getting. First, good luck in the race. I heard from Turner that you have a running partner?"

"A blind lady his brother knows. She needed someone…is that why you called?"

"I called about Oscar Swenberg."

Maile flipped back her sheet and sat crossed legged on her bed. After inspecting her toenails, she began massaging her feet. "What about him?"

"Remember I told you a while back that he left the hospital?"

"Yes, and I explained that he probably left AMA, against medical advice, because something upset him about his care or felt he couldn't pay his bill. For some reason, he felt he needed to leave the hospital."

"I checked on that. Shouldn't there be forms he'd have to sign? That's what the hospital told me, and he didn't. Plus, with his money, he'd have no problem paying his bill, or that of half the patients in the hospital."

"There would be just one form for him to sign, very simple, actually. They don't have something from him?"

"Nothing at all. They won't let me see his paperwork, though. Can I trust Honolulu Med for something like that?"

Maile started rubbing her other foot. "You're asking me because they fired me and went after my reputation as a nurse? Specifically, who did you talk to at the hospital?"

"His doctor and two of the nurses that took care of him back then. I made the point of going in to talk with each of them. They all told me the same thing, that it was a big surprise when he left. They made it sound like he didn't walk out with his middle finger in the air, but that he snuck out without anyone noticing. How is that possible? It seems to me that hospital corridors are busy places."

"They are, even in the middle of the night." She stretched her legs out in front of her and reached for her toes to stretch her legs. "What time of day did he leave?"

"Somewhere between ten-thirty and midnight. Would that be a good time to skip out?"

Maile leaned more pressure on one side than the other to stretch the muscles down the back of her leg. "Perfect time. The evening shift nurses would've taken the last set of vital signs and given evening meds while the night shift nurses were just coming on. I bet it was a night shift nurse that found an empty bed?"

"Right. She was one of the nurses I talked to. She'd gotten report on him, and when she went in to make rounds, his bed was empty. The strange thing was that the bed was made very neatly, almost as though he had tried to hide the fact it had been used all day."

Maile leaned her weight on the other leg to stretch those muscles. "Neatly with hospital corners?"

"I didn't ask, but the nurse said the bed was made the way it would be at someone's home. The entire room had been tidied, the water emptied from the jug and the plastic drinking cup clean and dry. He even folded his hospital gown and left it on the bed."

"What about his IV?" she asked.

"They found the tubing and bag of fluid in the bathroom trash. Is that hard to take out?"

"Not really. He'd need to wear a Band-Aid on his arm for a while. If they found the hospital gown he was wearing, that means he left in his own clothes, and likely had help. Did he have visitors that evening?"

"It was an evening when our hometown college football team was playing in a bowl game on TV, and everybody was watching that."

"It happens that way sometimes." Maile felt a kink in her rear end soften when she found a yoga position. "When there's some big event on TV, families come in to watch in patient rooms."

"Just so they can watch with the patient the way they would at home?" Ota asked.

"More like they can't get the game on TV at home. Patients generally don't care about watching TV. It's the visitors who watch. Had he been watching the game? I ask because that might give you a hint about who was visiting him that evening."

"I'll have to go back and ask. Are you okay?"

"I'm fine. Why?"

"You're panting and groaning. Am I interrupting a distraction?"

"I wish. I could use some distraction this evening."

"Want me to send Turner by?" Ota asked.

Maile went back to rubbing a knuckle into the sole of a foot. "He's back in my doghouse."

"Why?"

"Miss Wong."

"I explained earlier that she was arrested during a sting operation that Turner was an integral part of."

"Except you didn't see them before she was arrested. The way they looked so chummy, I would've guessed they been integrating quite often, including this morning before they arrived at the potluck."

"I'll have to check with him about that. You have a ride to the race in the morning?"

"Brock is picking Amelia and me up, along with Brian, I suppose. Thanks, though. Did you take Susan shopping?"

"There's a woman who knows how to shop. Thanks for the gift card, by the way. That took some of the heat off my credit card."

Maile gave up on rubbing muscles and covered up with the sheet. "Oh, listen to Daddy talk about his daughter being a grown up woman."

"I just wish she wasn't so grown up, if you know what I mean."

"And that's something you need to move on from as much as she needs to. But who am I to lecture a father about parenting? All I know is that I need to get some sleep."

Chapter Four

Maile was awake and dressed in her running outfit before her four AM alarm time. She was just finishing her second mug of coffee and third doughnut when the alarm chimed. Finishing her breakfast and washing it down with half a bottle of mango juice, she took her third mug of coffee with her downstairs to wait for Brock to pick her up for the quick ride to the marathon start line.

Amelia and Brian were in the back seat of his quad cab pickup. When Maile got in and greeted them, Amelia yawned while fixing her blond hair into a messy ponytail. Maile was a little surprised, that she had figured the woman would've approached the race more professionally, buttoned down and ready to go. To her eye, it looked a little like Amelia and Brian had spent a late night together, rather than getting a good night of sleep.

"You look nice," Brock said to Maile as he drove.

"Save it for Miss Wong."

"What's with the hostility?"

"What's with Miss Wong?" Maile muttered.

"She's in jail, awaiting transfer to a more secure facility. I heard Ota talked to you last night about her?"

"Yeah, sorry. He explained everything. Still just a sore spot. Just a little jealous."

"Of someone in jail?" he asked.

"Strange, huh? But that's what women think about late at night. No matter what, we never quite measure up to the competition, even if they are criminals."

"You look nice anyway."

"Thanks. Because I'm wearing tight running clothes and most of my body is exposed?"

"That helps. Never seen your hair like that."

She bundled the long braid into one knot and secured it with a scrunchie. "Don't get used to it."

"Why not?"

"Major pain in the neck to fix it like this." Maile put on her wide-brimmed visor hat, cinched it tight in back, and secured that with several bobby pins. "Ready to run, Amelia?"

"Not yet, but I will be."

"Only about half an hour before the starting gun goes off. We should try to work our way to the front to get a decent start."

"Could've started this a couple hours later," Amelia said, now sticking on her hat and adjusting it.

"Supposed to be a bright and sunny day, which means it'll get warm in a hurry."

Brock lifted Maile's mug. "How much coffee have you had this morning?"

"Enough to get me to mile thirteen. Then I'll be looking for a roving barista."

With the flood of runners and spectators streaming toward the start line, Brock got them as close as he could before parking. "Okay, the two of you are on your own. Good luck."

Maile stretched a little more while waiting for Amelia to get a last minute hug and pep talk from Brian. When Brock came around to Maile, she put her hand up to stop him.

"Already have my own pep talk and affirmations going internally."

"How about a hug for good luck?"

Maile wanted to make one last wisecrack about Miss Wong, but knew it would send her mood plummeting. Instead, she accepted his hug.

"Thanks, brah. I needed that," she said after they had separated again.

"How about another after the race?"

"Depending on how it goes, I might be cranky after, and in a lot of pain. Approach at your own risk."

"Not a good time to ask, but we still need to have our third date," he said.

"I'm still not convinced our first two encounters were actually dates. Might be best if we started over."

Brock's face brightened. "We'll compare schedules and find something."

"Oh, now doesn't that sound romantic?" Maile said, laughing. "Do Amelia and I get a ride home?"

"Only if you finish. Brian and I will be at the finish line watching for both of you."

Maile's body was groped until her hand was found, and she was given her end of the leash by Amelia to attach to her own wrist. "Somehow, I think we'll be together when the time comes."

"You and me?" Brock asked.

Maile patted his chest. "That's a marathon that needs to be run another time. But first, Amelia and I need to run today's marathon."

It was still dark as the race official made announcements over a loud speaker, and contestants chatted nervously as they waited for the starting horn.

Maile worked her way through the crowd to get as close to the front as possible, tugging Amelia along behind her. Once they were settled in the midst of the giant mass of humanity, Maile straightened Amelia's race number and *BLIND* bib. Amelia was wearing digital camo colored running clothes and visor, with *ARMY* stenciled across the top of her shirt. It was obvious who her main sponsor was. Maile spent another moment or two fixing her partner's visor hat and repositioned bobby pins. Amelia yawned the entire time.

"You awake?" Maile asked.

"Awake enough."

"Any last minute suggestions?" Maile asked, now stretching her legs the same way everyone else was, by pulling up her foot up behind her butt.

"Just keep up." Amelia yawned again. "If you can't keep up, cut me loose and stay out of the way."

As the race official called out a countdown to the start, Maile took several deep breaths, more to settle her nerves than for the air. When the horn blared, Amelia took off like a shot, yanking on the leash that bound them together. Maile caught a toe stumbling slightly, and needed several hurried steps to catch up.

"How's our pace?" Amelia asked when her sports watch chimed just as they passed the first mile mark.

"Okay," Maile breathed. "Seems a little forced for this early."

"This is my pace for the first five miles if I want to hit a four hour run."

"Okay."

"Then for the next fifteen miles, we'll take fifteen seconds a mile off."

"Okay. What about the last six miles?" Maile asked.

"Then we go back to the pace we're running now for the next five miles."

"What about the last mile?"

"Run, walk, crawl. Whatever gets us across the finish line."

"At this pace, that might start at around mile ten," Maile mumbled, as she sucked air more vigorously than she was expecting for so early in the race.

"You said you wanted to try for a sub-four hour marathon. This is your best bet to get it."

To Maile's ears, Amelia was beginning to sound like a drill sergeant. As it was, she was still trying to match strides and arm swings so the leash wasn't tugging back and forth between them so much. Amelia had a shorter arm swing, which Maile had to match, along with a shorter but faster stride.

"Yea, sure, four hours. Might have to get a longer leash for that. Like an hour longer."

They passed the three-mile mark, Amelia's watch chiming at the exact moment it should.

"What're you thinking about right now?" Amelia asked.

"I don't know. Just wondering how painful those middle fifteen miles will be."

"Get your mind of that and think of something else altogether."

"Like what?"

"What do you normally think about on long runs?"

"I usually make up algebra word problems. I try to figure out how many grams of sugar I'm using at my current pace, and how much Gatorade I need to drink to cover it, that sort of thing."

Amelia laughed. "Okay, forget all that nonsense, because that'll only make you thirsty. What's your biggest problem this week?"

"Finishing this race while still attached to you."

They ran along for a moment, huffing and puffing. At least their respiratory rates matched.

"Something besides running."

"Not really a problem, but maybe a little algebraic, is what happened to a man that disappeared from a hospital bed."

Maile slowed them down to make their first stop at a hydration station. She got several cups of red Gatorade for Amelia, before chugging down some herself. Grabbing two bananas, she peeled one and handed it to her partner after they started running again. Their pause lasted barely fifteen seconds.

"Why was he in the hospital?" Amelia asked, after tossing away her banana peel. Maile waved an apology when the peel landed in the lap of a spectator seated in a patio chair.

"He'd been hit by a car, but had been discharged. Later, he had setbacks of some sort and needed to be readmitted. He was being worked up for some unknown ailment, at least unknown to the police."

"Is this that Swenberg guy?"

"Yeah. You know about him?" Maile asked. They'd begun their faster pace, and she was already feeling the burn in her thighs.

"Brock was telling Brian and me about him. It's being treated as a simple missing person case, right?"

"It's a little more complicated than that."

"Why are you involved?" Amelia asked.

"Long story." Between huffs and puffs, Maile told her about the three Swenberg brothers, and how two of them were dead, and the third was now missing from the hospital. "That accident was more than suspicious."

"How?" Amelia asked.

"He'd tangled with organized crime gangsters over big loans that had never been paid back."

"I thought he was wealthy? Why'd he need the loans?"

"It was his girlfriend, wife, whoever she is, that needed the money. When she wasn't able to pay it back, the gangsters came after Carl."

"He couldn't just pay them off?"

"Not so easy, apparently. Not like I'm an expert about that stuff," Maile said. For some odd reason, either the conversation was taking her mind off her legs, or it was regulating her breathing better, and she wasn't suffering so much. "The police are still trying to determine the gangsters' roles in the deaths of Carl's brothers. The whole thing has been tragic."

"Sounds like it. What happened to the wife?" Amelia asked.

"Good question. The police are trying to figure out if she helped Carl leave the hospital, or if someone else did." Maile took several more breaths before continuing. "She's a walking soap opera all of her own."

"How does all of that involve you?"

"I was in either the right place or the wrong place a couple of times, when I rescued his brothers from drowning and poisoning. Somehow, Oscar and his wife are involved in those deaths, maybe as much as the gangsters are, but the police can't figure out exactly how. Now he's missing."

"And the police think you might be able to help?" Amelia asked.

"I think they think I know more than what I'm letting on."

"That you might be hiding him?"

"Or at least know where he is," Maile said. She wanted to make a polite request to ease back on the pace, but Amelia seemed more dedicated to the chime on her watch than to the fatigue in their legs. As it was, Maile wasn't sure why they needed to be tethered, since Amelia seemed to pass others at will, and without any guidance. That's when it dawned on her about the conversation. It was Amelia's way of letting other runners around them know they were about to pass. "I have no idea where he might be, and honestly, I don't care. I'm done with that whole drama."

"I heard a reward was being offered," Amelia said.

"Oh? How much?"

"I heard five figures. I wish I knew more about the case. If I did, I'd go after that reward."

"Well, let's figure it out as we run, and I'll share it with you."

"Great! A mystery to solve! Tell me more about Swenberg."

"He's fairly wealthy, with a house and yacht in Hawaii Kai. His wife is young, even younger than I am, and pretty. Very Hollywood. In fact, she went there for a few years in a quest to become an actress."

"Did she?" Amelia asked.

"Other than making a few pornos, no. That's what the loans to her were about, to buy her way into exposure."

Amelia chuckled. "If she was making pornos, she got exposure."

"Maybe not the kind she wanted. The last I heard, she's in rehab for an alcohol problem, but that was a few weeks ago. I doubt she has much to do with Oscar disappearing."

"You said both his brothers are dead?"

"Yep. It just seems to me that trouble finds Oscar more easily it does the rest of us. With or without his brothers, his wife, or the gangsters that tend to hang around him, he finds his way into trouble."

"I'm putting it on his wife," Amelia said.

"Why?"

"Men aren't smart enough to get into real trouble by themselves. They need us for that," Amelia said, just as her watch chimed. Another mile was under their belts. "Okay, that's ten miles. We've passed everybody that we can for at least the next five miles. Maybe we should shut up and concentrate on breathing and pace."

"Yeah, pace," Maile muttered.

"You're doing great, Maile."

"I am?"

"Just keep it up."

At mile fifteen, the crowd was thin, and Maile wondered why she still needed to guide her partner. The only runners being passed then were the ones who'd been rabbits, taking their early pace too fast and were now dropping out. Maile looked back and saw many more runners behind them than in front. She also sensed

Amelia beginning to tire. As it was, they were getting into the territory of Maile's longest runs. She was feeling good, though, and her feet were holding up. That had been her biggest worry, that she'd develop a blister that needed to be lanced along the way, and that would ruin Amelia's scientifically-planned marathon. Cramps weren't attacking her legs yet, either. All in all, she had nothing to complain about, especially considering they were still on track to break a four hour marathon, a monumental feat for a blind runner, and for a first-time marathoner.

At mile twenty, they were alone on the street, no one within a hundred yards before or after them. Spectators applauded and cheered them on as they ran past, giving Maile the mental boost she direly needed. Amelia seemed to be in a zone as her alarm chimed. Their pace didn't slow according to plans, though, and Maile did her best to match her stride with her partner's. While Amelia was maintaining the exact same pace as she had throughout the race, her stride never shortened either. Maile was internally begging for a shorter stride now, worrying about the blisters that were starting on her feet and the thigh muscles that were threatening to cramp. Seeing the determination on Amelia's face, she decided to keep quiet and keep her legs churning.

"Getting some blisters," Maile said when she couldn't help the limp that was starting in one leg.

"I've had them for five miles. Suck it up."

They did another mile. Spectators were getting thicker along the sides of the route, cheering on the runners as they passed. Maile barely noticed them now, and Amelia seemed oblivious.

"Getting a cramp in my hamstring."

"Shorten your stride a few inches and increase your pace slightly."

It took a couple hundred yards before Maile found something that worked, or at least wasn't as painful.

"Seriously, these blisters…"

"Forget the blisters. Run through them. They'll still be there at the end, one way or another."

They had two and a quarter miles to go and had been running for three hours and eighteen minutes.

"I think my watch is wrong."

"How so?" Amelia asked.

"Three hours and fifteen minutes and we have only two more miles to go."

"We're on track."

"We're on track for eight minute, forty second miles." Maile did some mental calculations. "That's a three and a half hour marathon."

"I told you we were going to do a sub-four hour race."

"I was thinking three-fifty nine!"

"You want to quit?"

"No."

"Then suck it up, sister. I don't need you turning into an anchor."

Maile watched as they approached the giant timer that spanned the finish line. She felt Amelia slowing, tugging back on the leash. She was now limping more than Maile.

"You okay?"

"How far are we?"

"Three hundred yards. Can you get there?"

"If I have to crawl, I'll get there. And I'm pretty close to that right now."

Amelia had been harping at Maile all morning about keeping up. It was now time to return the favor. She removed the leash and put her hand on Amelia's back to push a little.

"Just keep going. I'm not getting this close to a three and a half hour marathon and then lose it at the end."

For the first time, Amelia's face cracked and tears began to flow when she had to hop on one leg because of a cramp. Not doing any better, Maile went to her partner and got her arm over her shoulder. She felt the weight of Amelia transfer over to her legs.

"Come on. We've gone this far. We can do it."

"How far?"

"Hundred yards."

"Time?"

"Three Twenty-nine and fifteen."

No one was ahead of them as they got closer to the finish, only spectators and race officials. They were all clapping and yelling, urging them on to the end of the race. Maile saw the medical tent off to one side, with a couple of dead-tired runners being helped into it by volunteers. They had forty-five seconds to cover the last hundred yards if they wanted to crack the 3 ½ hour mark. They were hopping as much as they were running. When Maile felt Amelia's legs begin to run again, she matched her stride.

"Fifty yards, Amelia."

"Time?"

"Twenty-five more seconds."

Amelia's shortened stride broke again. When she began to do a hop-skip, Maile had to slow to stay with her.

"Run it out, Maile. I can make it from here."

"Forget that. We've gone this far together. I'm not leaving you behind."

That seemed to inspire Amelia and she hurried her skipping. Maile pushed her along, prompting her with times. She saw Brock and Brian standing off to one side, cheering for them, but along with hundreds of others cheering, she wasn't able to pick out their voices.

"Five more steps and we're done!" Maile told her companion.

Those last few seconds felt like minutes. Once they were past the finish line, Amelia collapsed. Only seconds after she hit the ground, her watch chimed. She reached for it, but her shaking hands couldn't press the button to silence the alarm.

Maile knelt down, barely able to bend her legs. She stopped the alarm. "We did it."

"Three-thirty?" Amelia asked, aiming her face at Maile.

"Three twenty-nine and eighteen seconds."

A tiny smile crossed Amelia's face as she set her head down on the ground.

Medical volunteers rushed out to Amelia and helped her into the first aid tent. Maile limped along after them, looking for a place to fall over.

Chapter Five

Once Maile had something to drink and was feeling up to it, she went to a table with fruit and Gatorade and made a couple of plates. Her legs were already stiffening up, and her feet were throbbing and swelling inside her shoes. Taking a plate to Amelia, she found her with an IV in her arm giving her fluids and in a lot of pain. A volunteer was just finishing taking her blood pressure.

"You're beginning to perk up a little. Your running partner is here with something to drink for you."

"Maile?" Amelia asked with a blank stare that seemed even more empty than usual.

"I have watermelon and cantaloupe for you, and grape Gatorade."

Amelia struggled to sit up a little. She took the watermelon Maile gave her and nibbled. "Are you mad at me?"

"A little. That was a dirty trick you played on me."

"I needed to do as well as I could to keep my sponsorship. I also needed a guide that might be able to keep up."

"What happened with your other guide? Tell me the truth," Maile demanded.

"She quit me a few days ago and ran the race on her own. She said I was too hard on her."

"You are pretty tough to deal with while running. The whole 'suck it up' bit is a little too much."

Amelia finished her bottle of Gatorade. "That's what I have to tell myself to get through these races. All I have to live on is my sponsorships, and those don't amount to much. Once I start slowing down or unable to finish a race, my sponsors will find someone else with more impressive results. And I can't run these races on my own. I don't know why people can't seem to understand that."

Maile decided to ease up a little. "Well, I wanted a good result, but I also wanted to have some fun with my first marathon. At least I got the result, and a much better one than I predicted."

"It's not fun running with me?" Amelia asked.

"Not much, no. But whatever. When's your next race?"

"This was the end of the season for me. I don't have to race until March. That's when I get busy again." After the nurse took the IV out of Amelia's arm, Maile helped her sit on the side of the cot. "Is Brian around?"

"Should be with Brock. Are you ready to leave?"

Arms over each other's shoulders, Maile and Amelia limped out of the tent together. Brock and Brian were waiting not far away. Maile needed to guide her partner into Brian's arms. Once they were hugging, or maybe it was Brian holding her up, Maile turned her attention on Brock.

"Three and a half hour marathon!" he said. "You guys came in third in the blind-with-guide category. Well done!"

"Tell my feet that," Maile said. She also wanted the bear hug that Amelia was getting. "And my legs, butt, back, and neck. You're giving me a ride home, right?"

"Let me drop them off first. She looks in worse shape than you."

Maile waited in the pickup truck while Brock helped Brian get Amelia up the stairs to their third floor apartment. There was a brief discussion about something between the brothers at the door before Brock left again.

"Your place or your mom's?" he asked, getting back in the pickup again.

"Mine. Mom would only scold me. I'm not sure she even watched."

"She was at the finish line with Reverend Ka'uhane and a few others. They left when they saw you go to the medical tent with Amelia. Why would she scold you for doing so well in the race?" he asked.

"For hurting myself. She's never been athletic and doesn't understand about needing to win, in spite of the pain it requires to do well."

"Is it more than just painful muscles?"

"You ever run a marathon?" she asked.

"Not even close."

"Then you have no idea how much pain is involved in crossing that finish line, or just sitting here."

"Not so easy then?" he asked.

"If marathons were easy, they wouldn't have so much mystique, and everybody would be doing them."

"What was the hardest part?"

"Dealing with Amelia." She eased her head back and closed her eyes. "What's the opposite of bliss? I found that at mile fifteen."

"You're a lot stronger than I am, Mai. Before I park, do you need anything from the store?"

"All I need is a shower and a bed. And a handful of painkillers."

Maile needed his help in getting up the single flight of stairs to her door. She handed over the keys so he could open it. Before she could get in, her neighbor's door opened and Rosamie came out. She had a pained looked on her face when she saw Maile.

"Did you do it?"

"Yep, I did it. It did me, too."

"Need my help with anything?" Rosamie asked.

Maile was too tired to smile. "Thanks. I have Brock to help me."

Rosamie's face brightened. "Yes, I think he can take better care of you than I can."

Brock helped her in and got the door closed before an inquisition could start. Maile limped to her bed and flopped onto her back. "What have I done?"

"You ran it too fast."

"Maybe. Do you mind taking my shoes and socks off? Please?" She felt the pain of them being removed, but the relief once they were off was paradise.

"Your feet are in bad shape, Mai. They're already starting to swell and you have blisters all over. You shouldn't have run so fast."

"I got the blisters from the shoes, not the speed. I got the sore muscles from both the miles. I would've had blisters and sore muscles even if I had run a five hour race like I originally planned."

"What do you want me to do?"

"Make a couple of sandwiches and find something to drink." She sat up again, with his help. "I need to take a shower and deal with twenty-six miles of sweat, spit, and Gatorade. Some of that spit's not even mine. The disgusting thing about that is, right now, I don't mind so much."

For once, there was plenty of hot water in the shower. She wanted the flow of cool water over her body, and by the time she was rinsing away suds, she was easing the water temperature up a little.

"Now I just need to get rid of Brock," she whispered, putting aloe on the sunburn she'd got during the race. She dressed in the loosest clothes she had and left the bathroom. Joining him at the little table, she took a couple bites of the sandwich he'd made and drank the milk. Leaving him at the table, she went back to her bed. She used her pillows to prop up her legs.

"My sandwich isn't good?" he asked.

"It's okay. I think everything needs to rest right now."

"You want me to go so you can sleep?"

"Honestly, I'm too tired to sleep. Or too wound up. Or in too much pain. I don't know what I am right now. Can you do me a favor? In the kitchen drawer next to the sink is a little sewing kit. Mind bringing it over?"

"You're going to sew something?" he asked, handing the small kit to her.

She was sitting cross-legged then, examining her feet. "Puncture some of these blisters."

He sat on the edge of the bed to watch. "Those look nasty."

"Hopefully, they'll stick down again." She told him where to find Band-Aids in the bathroom, and began wrapping flattened blisters. "I know it's asking a lot, but once I'm done with this, do you mind rubbing my feet a little?"

"As long as they're clean."

Maile eased back onto her mattress and let Brock begin. It was soft and gentle, exactly what she wanted. After a few more minutes, she needed more.

"Okay, grind a knuckle into the sole of my foot and rub it back and forth. That really gets the blood flowing. Just don't rub a blister. And turn on the fan."

Maybe it was her low blood sugar, or blood flowing through her legs again, or simply fatigue catching up with her, but Maile's mind began to swirl while Brock worked on her feet. By the time he was done with those, the over-the-counter pain pills were working, and she was finding some relief. At one point, she must've dozed off, because there was a snap of a dream in which she was running again, bringing her back to the here and now. She felt hands on her legs, massaging her calves.

"Brock?"

"Yes?"

"Too tired for anything more than a massage, brah."

"Not looking for anything more."

"Kinda feels like you are."

"Want me to stop?" he asked.

"No. Rub harder. Feel those baseballs in my calves? Those used to be muscles. See if you can get those to soften a little." There was more pain than pleasure as he worked on the knots in her legs, too much to allow her to doze off again. For some reason, she thought of Oscar Swenberg. Staring at the water stain on the ceiling over her bed, she started a conversation to get her mind off the pain. "Hey, why is Ota so concerned about Swenberg being missing?"

"It's a missing person case that was assigned to him. He has to investigate. That's the job of a detective, to be concerned."

"Those Swenbergs have been a pain in the neck since the very first moment I met one of them."

"I think he feels the same way. Down to only one of them now, though."

"Don't forget Honey, or Laurie, whatever she goes by these days. I wonder how her rehab is going?"

"I heard she's getting out pretty soon, or might already be."

"What does someone do after rehab?" Maile said, as Brock started on her other calf.

"Find a place to live, get a job, move on from their trouble. Not much else can be done."

"She has that fancy house in Hawaii Kai to live in, and Oscar's bank account. All she has to do is hire a private detective to look for Oscar."

"Ota has been looking into their relationship. It turns out they aren't officially married, only together. No marriage license has ever been granted or paperwork filed, either here in Hawaii or in California where he's from originally."

"Didn't have a quickie in Vegas?"

"He probably checked on that, too. The other issue that gets people in trouble is that common law marriage isn't legal here in Hawaii, unless that marriage was declared in another state. California has very specific laws about common law. It would be up to lawyers and a judge to determine if Laurie Long is entitled to Oscar Swenberg's property here in Hawaii if their only claim to marriage was common law in California."

"And that would be assuming he's dead, right?" It was a risk since Maile was half in a daze, but she was willing to take that risk. "Maybe you could start on my quads?"

Brock began kneading one of her thighs. "If they are married, and if she's legally entitled to his property, she'd still have to wait for seven years to make a claim to it, if his body was never found."

"Why do you say body?"

"To legally prove death, an identifiable body is needed. Legally, people aren't dead until there is undeniable evidence of their death, and that requires a body. Or at least as much of their remains that death would be conclusive."

Maile winced as much from the pain Brock was inflicting on her leg as what he said. "But you're assuming he's dead."

He started on her other thigh. "I'm assuming nothing. I'm not the investigating officer on his case, Ota is."

Wanting a glass of wine to go with the massage, Maile closed her eyes. "I wonder what Honey…Laurie is going to do?"

"Not your problem, Mai. You owe her nothing. If anything, she and Swenberg owe you."

"At least an apology. I doubt I'll ever get it, though." Maile grabbed one of her pillows, fluffed it up and tossed it toward the head of the bed. With that, she turned over onto her belly. "Slave, work some of that magic on my hamstrings."

"Slave?" he said quietly.

Maile smiled into her pillow. "Yes, you heard me, slave. You're not getting any fancy ideas about taking advantage of me, are you?"

"What would you do if I tried?"

"My mother knows your mother."

"They can get their own slaves."

She looked back at him, now enjoying a sense of relaxation, even if her feet still throbbed. "I think you're done."

"With the massage?"

"I'm beginning to sense something in the works. You don't have to leave, though."

"I was hoping to stay."

"Oh, yes, Amelia and Brian have the bedroom, I suppose. Where have you been sleeping since she got there?"

"The couch."

"I've been on that couch." Maile thought of the time recently when she was at Brock's apartment, visiting with Brian. She'd been playing an odd bridal party game that involved kissing strangers, and had gotten a good one from Brian. She wondered ever since if that secret had ever been shared between the brothers. "What I mean is, I've sat on that couch. As you can see, I don't have a couch. I don't even have a good chair for you to sleep in."

He set his hand on the small of her back. "Yeah, that's a problem."

"We haven't even had our third date yet."

"We've had two?"

"I'm counting the trip to Swenberg's house and yacht as our first date. If we had to get that dressed up, it was a date, even if the police department thinks it was an undercover investigation."

"And the second?" he asked.

"Dinner the other night."

"That was with Ota and his daughter at Denny's."

"I've decided it's good enough for me after all."

"Pretty flimsy excuse for a date."

"So, I'm a cheap date."

Brock lay next to her on the double bed. "You don't seem like the kind of girl to offer herself before the third date."

Maile pushed up onto her side to face him. They were close enough that she could feel his warm breath on her cheek. "I'm not. We're in kind of a predicament, huh?"

"I don't suppose taking you to the marathon and bringing you home again could be considered a date?"

"Sorry. But giving me a massage might be."

"It was a massage without pretense."

"Maybe. But it did get a little personal a couple of times."

"What if I kissed you?"

"I'd have to defend myself."

He leaned forward and they kissed.

"I didn't think you'd resist."

"Too tired. If you do that again, you'll need to hold me." She touched the stubble on his face. "To keep me from resisting, of course."

This time, they held each other close, and shared the first passionate kiss she'd had in years. Once the moment passed and they relaxed again, Maile smiled at him.

"Is that how you kissed Miss Wong?"

He scooted back from her, his embrace not as tight. "What's your problem with her?"

"My problem is that she was doing her best to steal you away from me, even before I had a chance to chase after you."

"The times you saw us together were a part of that sting operation, that's all, Maile. She and a few others are now in jail awaiting trial because of the money laundering operation they were conducting in the restaurant."

"So, what happened, then? You kissed me goodbye late the other evening, and then showed up with her on your arm at the potluck the next morning."

"Even less happened with her than what happened between you and me on our first dates."

"The two of you looked awfully cozy that time I saw you at the falls," she said.

"All of which was instigated by her. Trust me, it wasn't easy writing that in a police report, even if nothing happened."

"You guys never…"

"Not at all. Not even this far."

"Okay."

"You do realize that I could be jealous of Robbie, right?"

She laughed. "Your only concern about him is that he survives the moment if I ever see him again."

Maile knew it was time to let go of Miss Wong, her ex-husband Robbie, too many petty jealousies, and move on. Pulling herself close to Brock, she gave him the kiss she'd been wanting from him for months.

Chapter Six

After Maile's morning shower, she dressed in the bathroom, wondering what she might have in cupboards to feed Brock for breakfast. Figuring she would need to take him somewhere, she gave up on the idea of being domestic that morning. When she went out and saw him at the kitchen counter, he already had his serious police officer look to his face.

"I'm expecting Detective Ota to bust through the door at any moment to arrest me."

"For what?"

She kissed his cheek. "Not taking advantage of one of his officers."

"Yeah, you dozed off just when it was getting fun," he said. "Am I really that boring?"

"Not usually. But it was the marathon that made me doze off. You were very charming. Keep trying." She finished drying her hair. "Otherwise, I'm done causing trouble for the police department."

He held up the several slips of paper he'd been reading. "You're in more trouble than that."

"Why?"

"Have these been paid?"

She grabbed the slips from his hand, stuffed them in a drawer, and slammed it shut.

"Not yet. They're just parking tickets."

"Some of them are old, and there were a couple of traffic citations in there, Maile. Where'd they all come from?"

"My glove compartment. I sold my car yesterday and those were still in it."

"You have to deal with those."

"They'll get paid, okay? Are we going to breakfast?"

He opened the drawer to look at the tickets again. "When?"

"People generally eat breakfast in the morning after getting up," she said while winding her hair into a knot.

"No, when will the tickets get paid?"

"Now that I have a little extra money in my bank account, this week. Are we walking to breakfast or are you driving?"

"How're your feet?"

"They've been better but I can walk a few blocks."

"How are the blisters?" he asked.

"Most of them are okay."

He tossed the citations down. "Speaking of Ota, I got a call from him while you were in the shower. He needs to meet with me about something. Are you okay to get something to eat on your own?"

There it was, every woman's nightmare ending to spending the night with a man. Even if they spent the night on the bed next to each other, they hadn't been together. Maile didn't know if she'd done something wrong that morning, if not having some sort of breakfast ready for him to eat, or if he really was upset with her over a handful of tickets. She doubted seriously that Detective Ota needed him. Brock hadn't said anything about Sunday being a workday for him. Or maybe it was as simple as dozing off while making out, never bringing that moment to completion. All she could do was watch him hurry down the hall on his way out of the building, and without her.

She slammed the door closed. "Boy, am I dumb. I haven't learned a thing about men."

While waiting for her tea to cool, she changed the Band-Aids on her heels and toes. After that, she changed into an outfit worthy of church. By the time she was sitting with her mother and brother in their pew, the memory of spending the night with Brock had soured. After Reverend Ka'uhane's last prayer to end the service, Maile made a fast break for the exit. One person she did notice not in attendance was Brock.

With a day off and nothing else better to do, she simply went home. Once she was there, she called Brian. She told herself it was to check on Amelia, but maybe there was another motive involved.

"She's doing okay? Did she get a good meal last night?"

"Giant, and has eaten breakfast twice," Brian said.

"How are her feet and legs?"

"I lanced the blisters I found, and I've been massaging her legs. I'll get her outside for a walk later."

"Yeah, she needs to keep moving to help her legs recover. But she knows better than I do about marathon recovery." Maile bit her lip, wondering if she should ask. "Is Brock around?"

"He never came in last night. Must've worked an overtime shift."

"Maybe. He's not there right now?"

"Not right now. Can I take a message? Or why don't you call him directly? I'm sure he'd like to hear from you."

"I get the idea I've taken up too much of his time lately."

"For you, he has time, Maile. Of that I'm certain."

"Maybe." After the call, she needed something to put her mind off Brock. "Okay, there's a reward for finding Oscar Swenberg. The best way to find him is through Honey…Laurie. She's in rehab somewhere. I wonder if they allow visitors in rehab? First, I have to find her."

She looked in the phone book for drug and alcohol rehabilitation centers and found three pages of them. Instead of calling every single one and likely getting told to get lost by all of them, she called Detective Ota. Once again, she might've had an ulterior motive.

"Why do you want to talk to her?" he asked.

"To see if she knows anything about Oscar."

"I've already been to see her twice, along with one or two other investigators. She's either clammed up tight about him, or she doesn't know anything."

"You talked to her as a cop. Maybe she'll open up to me."

"I never even talked to her directly. The staff at the center wouldn't let me in, saying she was still getting intensive therapy. The couple of minutes they spent on me gave me nothing new about her."

"Maybe they'll let me in."

"What's your angle?" he asked.

"To approach her as a friend. Where is she?"

"Look, you didn't get this from me, understand?"

Maile sighed. Some fatigue was beginning to set in again from the big run the day before, and it was affecting her mood as much as Brock was. "This is where I'm supposed to say 'who are you?' and we both laugh. Where is she?"

"Pali Rehab, Nu'uanu Valley, all the way up near the golf course. Small, private place in a house, individualized one-on-one care. You know how to get there?"

"Number thirteen bus turns around near there."

"You sure like our bus system. How'd the race go yesterday?" Ota asked.

"You haven't heard?"

"I saw a write-up about it in the newspaper this morning. They didn't mention your name as the winner."

"Disappointed?"

"A little. I know how hard you trained for it."

If Ota hadn't heard about the race, did that mean he hadn't seen Brock that morning?

"Detective, is Brock with you?"

"I'm at home. My daughter and I are catching up on the last few years. Need to talk to her about tomorrow?"

"She'll be fine. Just remind her to…"

"Dress appropriately?"

"And be on time. No idea where Brock is?"

"None. Why are you looking for him?" Ota asked.

"Honestly, I don't know why."

Transit service on Sundays wasn't as good as weekdays, but she had the last couple of miles to herself as the bus rumbled up the residential streets of Nu'uanu Valley. When she was as close to the rehab center as the bus got, she walked the last couple of blocks. It was a warm afternoon, and since her feet were beginning to throb again, she thought of the marathon the day before. She was still a little angry about being deceived by

Amelia, but she also knew she never would've got close to the same time if she hadn't been pushed so hard. She also knew it would be a long time before she ran another marathon.

The house that the rehab center occupied was large, modern, and secure. Palms and dense landscaping hid the front, while the back faced a large golf course. The other homes nearby were large, bordering on luxurious. Maybe Laurie Long was having personal problems in her life, but Maile knew she'd found her way into a wealthier lifestyle than that of her modest childhood.

After ringing the doorbell, Maile had to explain who she was to an intercom. Then she needed to do a little convincing that she knew Laurie Long was being treated there, and that they were acquainted. When asked to show a picture ID to a small video node that was a part of the intercom, she waved her driver's license. That reminded her she still had traffic ticket fines to pay, something she needed to figure out how to do and where to go. After a few minutes, she was let into the care center by an older woman. Dressed in drab clothes and wearing a boyish haircut, Maile wondered if she was a nun.

The woman introduced herself as Esther. She seemed angry about something. "You're here to see Laurie?"

"Yes. Is there a problem? Am I interrupting something?"

Esther led Maile to an office to talk privately. "No. It's just that she went out for a walk last evening at sunset and hasn't been back. She needs to realize that breaks her social contract with us."

"I don't know anything about her contract or the treatment she gets. I'm just here to visit her. Has she stayed out all night before?"

Esther shook her head. "She only recently got her privileges upgraded to outdoor activities. She wasn't supposed to be alone, but she convinced the evening staff that she'd be gone for only a moment to watch the golfers."

"I'm pretty sure golfers don't play golf in the dark."

"That's what I told them. Once sunset turned to dark, they started to worry and went looking for her."

"And they couldn't find her?" Maile asked.

"They checked at the country club, and knocked on neighbors' doors to see if she'd been invited in. Nothing."

"Did you report her as missing to the police?"

Esther shook her head again. "Officially, she's not missing. She was here voluntarily, and as far as I'm concerned, left the same way."

Maile wondered if Carl was somehow involved, that either he came for her, or had sent someone to get her. "Did anyone come to visit her yesterday that she might've made plans with to meet later last evening?"

"You're the first visitor she's had in weeks. Frankly, Miss Spencer, I'm still a little reluctant to talk about Laurie with you. It's more than a little suspicious that someone comes to visit only a few hours after she walked out. Not sure of what to make of that," Esther said.

Maile shifted nervously. She wasn't guilty of anything, but Esther had a way of making her feel that way. "Neither do I."

"Who are you to Laurie again?"

"We were friends, acquaintances in high school. Then a while back our paths crossed again and we reconnected."

Esther tipped her hand with the direction her attitude was going by sneering slightly. "You knew her in Hollywood?"

"No, I only know of her life here in Honolulu. I know she found some trouble in California a while back, and I just wanted to say hello, offer some support. That's all."

"It's not uncommon for friends to bring drugs to residents, but with the way you look, I doubt you'd do something like that."

Maile felt almost insulted with Esther's insinuation that she was too clean and wholesome to be diabolical. "I'm not here to bring her drugs. I only want to say hello, ask a few questions, and offer some support."

Esther shuffled papers and files around on her desk. "Well, she walked out last night without saying a word to anyone if she was coming back. I'm already looking for a new occupant for her room."

"And that means she could go whenever she wanted?" Maile asked. "Wouldn't she have to check out, or at least let someone know she wasn't coming back?"

"That would be optimal, yes. But not necessary. You do realize that she'll still be billed for her visit?"

"Paying her bill isn't my problem. My problem is needing to talk to her about Oscar."

"Oscar?"

"Yes, her husband."

"Husband?" Esther asked.

"Apparently, it was a common law marriage that started in California. Or maybe just partners. No one's quite sure, which is a big sticking point for those of us trying to find Oscar. And now Laurie."

"I'm sorry, Miss, but one of us is terribly confused. Who are you looking for again?"

"Laurie Long, also known as Honey Thrust. That was the actress name she used in Hollywood."

"I don't know who those others are, but Laurie Long has been staying with us for several months." Esther opened a metal file cabinet and retrieved what looked like a thick patient chart that would be used in a hospital. After leafing through several pages, she finger-read a few lines and put the file away again. "Yes, she was first admitted six months ago."

"Six months?" Maile asked. The math didn't add up. She'd seen Laurie more recently than that. "I just saw her about two months ago. Sure, she needed rehab then, but hadn't checked in yet."

While Esther returned Maile's gaze, she seemed to clean her teeth with multiple sweeps of her tongue. "This is a very complicated situation."

Maile tried a different question. "Even more so for me. Is she here or not?"

Esther got up and opened the office door. "Come with me."

Maile didn't know where she was being taken, but she obeyed. The house was larger than she expected, and after going through another locked door, she found it arranged more like a nursing home than a private residence. No one was seated in the small living room. Going past the first bedroom, she peeked in. One patient was in a bed, but instead of wearing pajamas or casual wear, he was hooked up to a respiratory ventilator, a nurse standing guard over him, a clipboard in her hand. The same scene was played out in the next room, and every room thereafter, until Esther led her into a patient room. She went to the opposite side of the bed, allowing Maile to stand at the other.

"Ms. Spencer, this is Laurie Long."

Maile looked at the young woman first through curiosity. But with the endotracheal tube protruding from the hole in the front of her neck, and the body covered with a patient gown and sheet, the nursing part of her brain kicked in. She looked at the name band on the patient's wrist, and at the name on the chart the attendant nurse was holding. She looked again at the young woman in the bed. She was Asian, slender, and had a dye job in her hair that had grown out several inches. She was a good match, but not quite right.

"This isn't the Laurie Long I'm looking for."

"How do you know?"

"First, let me ask why she has a tracheostomy and is intubated?"

"Overdose that led to a stroke that almost killed her. She's been in a vegetative state ever since. She also has a feeding tube to her stomach. The family is unwilling to let her go, so, she's here. I don't know for how much longer, though."

"Why?" Maile asked.

"Pneumonia that won't get better and she's thrown at least one clot. Bless her heart, because that's the only thing keeping her alive," Esther said quietly.

"This place isn't a drug and alcohol rehab center? That's the assumption the police have, and how you advertise in the yellow pages, and online."

"We started out that way several years ago, but this is more profitable. Also, the neighbors prefer these patients over the previous ones."

"Why?" Maile asked.

"In the past, there were times when visitors became disruptive in the neighborhood. We still use the same name, and would rather not advertise our real intent. People make up cruel names for our patients. Hospitals know us, though, and send patients when we have vacancies."

"You told me a few minutes ago that Laurie left last night, that she walked out on her own accord. Why'd you tell me that?"

"We get people here occasionally, investigative journalists poking around places they shouldn't, and angry family members thinking we should've worked a miracle by waking up their loved one. Miracles don't happen here, Ms. Spencer."

"Okay, fine. But this isn't the Laurie Long the police are interested in. She fits the general physical description, but this isn't her."

"How can you be sure?" Esther asked.

"Look at her. This woman would wear a thirty-four B bra size, right? But the real Laurie Long had plastic surgery a couple of years ago, and was built entirely different than this woman."

"You're sure about that?"

"I saw them myself once. Plus, Laurie has a tattoo on a hip. Does this woman?" Maile asked the nurse.

The nurse shook her head. "I've seen every square inch of her and she has no tattoos at all."

"That's not her face, either," Maile said. "They could be sisters or cousins, but that's not her. Where does this woman's family live?"

"The one time they came to visit, they said they live in Honolulu. That's her permanent address."

That didn't fit with where Laurie had lived with Oscar. She wondered if she could be wrong, that the girl in the bed really was her old acquaintance. She was pale, skinny, and terribly sickly, which changes everyone's appearance. Maybe a little impulsively, she pulled the sheet back and lifted the girl's gown to see her breasts. They were what she would expect of a young Asian woman, and had no scars as though implants had been put in and later removed. Other than the degradation that bodies undergo in long-term rehabilitation, and the rubber feeding tube that was securely taped to her belly, she was an attractive young woman, but built nothing like the Laurie Long Maile had seen a few weeks before.

The nurse covered the girl's body again.

"Does the name Swenberg mean anything to you?" Maile asked.

Esther and the nurse looked at each and both shrugged. "Never heard of them."

"Are you sure? You've already misled me once."

"This woman was admitted directly from the hospital with the name of Laurie Long. The chartwork that was sent with her also had that name. The family visited that same day and identified themselves as the Long family." Esther's previous sneer had changed to something of confusion.

"What was the history of the overdose?" Maile asked.

The nurse answered. "She'd just returned from living in LA. The family said she'd turned into a party girl. I guess she kept up that lifestyle. They said one night she collapsed in a nightclub and was rushed to the hospital. She'd suffered a massive stroke from all the drugs she'd taken. Too bad for her family she didn't die."

"That sounds like something that could've happened to the Laurie I know," Maile said quietly. She felt bad then, talking about the young woman in the bed the way they were, as though she was simply a case study and not a person. She looked at her face again. The girl's brows needed to be plucked, the dye job was long past looking attractive, her complexion was pale, and her lips were chapped. Even with all that, she was convinced she wasn't the woman she was looking for. "Sorry, but I think somebody has made a terrible mistake."

"Who's this?" Esther asked, looking back and forth at Maile and the nurse, a look of consternation on her face,

Maile left the room. "I have no idea."

As soon as she was outside, she had to pop up her umbrella against a shower that was starting. Her feet were throbbing more than ever from being on them all day, but she continued down the hill to the next bus stop. Getting out her phone, she called Detective Ota.

"You have a problem."

Chapter Seven

"What do you mean, Laurie Long isn't there?" Detective Ota demanded.

"Not the one we know from Oscar Swenberg's house in Hawaii Kai. Pali Rehab is no longer a treatment center for alcohol recovery. It's a long-term treatment facility for patients that need mechanical ventilation but not hospitalization. Those places are often called rehab centers."

"Aren't those patients unconscious?"

"Generally, yes. Or paralyzed and require too much care for the family to offer."

"They could've told me that when I visited the other day."

"Esther? She lied to me initially, until finally coming clean after I pressured her. It's amazing what a staring contest can accomplish. She even took me to a patient's room with who they think is Laurie Long."

"I take it the patient wasn't?" he asked.

"Close match, but not close enough."

"How do you know? It's been a while since you've seen her, and you told me once that patients look entirely different in a hospital bed than they do ordinarily. You were even talking about a Swenberg then."

"First, I was told this woman has been there for six months. Plus, the Laurie we know had breast augmentation surgery, but not the girl in the rehab center."

"How do you know?"

"I looked. No scars. Just average-sized…whatever. Laurie has a tattoo on one hip, but not the girl I saw. The nurse taking care of her confirmed she has no tattoos on her body anywhere."

"Maile, you need to work for the police department."

"Why?"

"Because you'd be the best investigator we'd have."

"There's something peculiar going on there, though."

"Why do you think that?" he asked.

"At first, Esther tried telling me Laurie walked away last night and never came back."

"That's the same thing Oscar did."

"Then she explained that away by saying patients are allowed to leave whenever they want since they're all there on a voluntary basis. But there's no way any of them could possibly walk out."

"Because of being paralyzed or incapacitated?"

"Exactly. She lied to both of us."

"I'll send someone to collect fingerprints from the patient in the bed," Ota said.

"The other problem is that Esther knew nothing about Oscar Swenberg when I mentioned his name. So, she's either lying about a whole lot of things, or she's really clueless."

"Might be another explanation. I'll call you back. That's assuming you're interested in helping me with Oscar?"

"I heard something about a reward," Maile said.

"And I heard something about a substantial deposit in your bank account recently."

"Not yet. And to take a phrase from your vocabulary, I'm not counting my chickens before they hatch."

"I say that?"

"I've heard you say it couple of times." Her throbbing feet reminded her of Brock for some reason. "Hey, how much trouble is there if tickets don't get paid?"

"Your credit rating sinks, and you could end up in court. Why?"

"I don't suppose it's possible to have them fixed, is it? Is that what it's called, fixing a ticket?"

"Yes, and no, it's not possible. How many do you have?" he asked.

"I think there's eight, but only two are traffic tickets, and one of the others was from the airport. Does that matter?"

"It only matters if you want to stay out of jail. I know how much you enjoy a trip to the women's cellblock."

Maile ended the call before making a wisecrack about his daughter Susan, but as owner of her small tour company, she needed the girl as a guide. She hadn't noticed that she walked right past one bus stop and was just getting to the next one when the bus came to a stop.

Laurie could be anywhere on Oahu, maybe hiding from the police, maybe just hanging out with Oscar. There was no way for Maile to know if she was even still in the islands.

"Unless…"

Maile went to the internet on her phone and found a useful 'people finder' site. She put in Laurie's name and waited a moment. Three addresses came up, Oscar's in Hawaii Kai, an address in Hollywood, and an address near the high school they both had attended. She never did know why, but a few streets in that area were named Elm, Birch, and Alder, trees that typically didn't grow in Hawaii. Putting the Long family address to memory, she watched for the closest bus stop to it. When it came, she gingerly stepped down to the sidewalk.

"Why am I doing all this walking the day after a marathon? I could have my feet up at my mother's house, sipping iced tea."

It was a long block to walk to find the house. Twice the size as her mother's cottage, it filled most of the lot. The only landscaping was a large avocado tree in the front yard and a narrow walkway to the front porch. She let herself in through the gate.

Even if the front yard was sparse, the house was in good shape, with new paint, clean windows, and a sturdy-looking porch. Coming from a window was the sound of a whirring air conditioner. On either side of the lowest step was a stone lion standing guard for the entrance. The screen door was propped open, and a red sheet of paper was stuck to the closed door. Maile recognized it as some sort of good luck charm used by Chinese people, usually around the New Year holiday. A vertical sign was next to the door, completely in Chinese.

When she knocked, she heard small footsteps trot through the house on hardwood floors. After a moment, the door eased open and a pair of eyes peeked out at her. A little girl spoke a few words, something Maile couldn't understand. With that, she figured the address she'd found for Laurie's family was too old to be reliable. When she started to turn to leave, someone else spoke to her.

"May I help you?" a young man asked.

"Maybe. I was looking for the Long house."

"We're the Longs. Which one do you want?"

"Laurie, if she still lives here? It looks like I might be in the wrong place."

The door opened a little more. "You a social worker?"

Maile shook her head. "An old friend. We knew each other in high school."

The young man, not much more than a teenager, postured the way Maile's brother would when acting tough. "You look like the social workers that used to come around."

"I'd just like to say hello, see how she's doing."

"She's not here."

"Will she be home soon?" Maile asked.

"I doubt it. Who are you again?" the young man asked.

"I'm Maile Spencer."

"Oh, you." An elderly Chinese woman came to the door, and the young man spoke to her in Chinese for a moment, nodding his head at Maile. "What do you want with Laurie?"

"I already told you, I just wanted to talk with her for a few minutes. Is she here?"

"Not anymore."

"Will she be back soon?"

"Kinda doubt it," he said.

"Do you know where I might find her?"

"Do I look like her personal secretary?" the young man asked.

After looking Maile up and down, the woman elbowed the young man and spoke in Chinese to him, finishing with a smile to Maile.

"My grandmother wants to invite you in."

"Well, if Laurie's not here…"

As if the grandmother had the final say in everything, he opened the door completely and stepped back. Once she was in, Maile kicked off her shoes and left them with all the others scattered around the entrance. The house was cool, a result of the air conditioner that was running somewhere. She was led to a tiny living room, with just two small sofas positioned at angles to each other, with a small marble table in front of them. She was pointed to a sofa and left alone.

"Now what?" Maile whispered after a few minutes of listening to the young man play with a toddler, the little girl's playful voice echoing down a hall. Checking her watch, she needed to find a polite way out of the house. As it was, Maile wasn't sure if she was sitting there until Laurie returned from somewhere, or if there was some misunderstanding.

The old woman returned with a tray with a kettle and several cups. Steam rose from the spout as she poured two cups of green tea. She handed one to Maile.

"Thank you."

With even more confusion over what was going on right then, Maile and the elderly woman sat in silence as they sipped the aromatic blend of tea. It wasn't simple green tea that Maile drank occasionally, but had other flavors in it. Hoping it wasn't spiked with something, she finished most of her cup and set it down again.

The old woman picked up Maile's abandoned cup and looked at the loose leaves at the bottom. She gave it a swirl and watched as they settled. Holding out the cup for Maile to see the leaves, the old lady launched into a lecture about something in Chinese, at once smiling, and then frowning, before smiling about something again.

Wondering if more parlor tricks were to follow, she listened to footsteps clomp up the steps and come in. A woman spoke Chinese to anyone that might've been listening, which wasn't the elderly woman with Maile, at least not that she could see. The woman had several grocery bags in her hands when she came into the room. She stopped suddenly when she saw Maile seated there.

"I didn't know we were expecting a guest."

Maile stood. "I'm sorry. I'm interrupting your home. I just came by to see if Laurie still lived here."

Taking over as hostess, the woman went through the same question and answer quiz as earlier before she went to another room with the grocery bags. The elderly woman went with her. The young man was called for, creating a three-way discussion about something in Chinese, with the occasional English phrase thrown in, almost as if they were trying to keep Maile's attention. While all that went on, Maile noticed the little girl had returned, only to peek around a corner, watching Maile. A few minutes later, the middle-aged woman returned, sat, and poured two more cups of tea.

"Why are you looking for Laurie?"

"To say hello, see how she's doing," Maile said.

"My son said you're her new social worker. I thought we were done with the lot of you."

"I'm not a social worker." It was time to tell the truth. "I need to talk to her about Oscar Swenberg."

The woman stiffened. "Oh. You're with the police."

"No, just looking on my own."

"Nobody cares about my daughter. Worst day of her life when she met Oscar."

"Maybe so."

"How do you know her again?"

"High school. She took my place in the cheerleading squad when I graduated."

"Oh, yes. I think I remember you now. What's so important about Swenberg that he needs to be brought back into anyone's life?"

"Just to find out where he is, if he's even still alive."

"We'd all like to be left alone, at least when it comes to Swenberg. We've had enough of his trouble."

"As I have. Do you know where he is? Or if he's still alive?"

"I don't see why you're looking for Oscar if you want nothing more to do with him?" the woman asked.

"I suppose a social worker would call it closure."

The woman set down her cup, a few leaves drifting at the bottom. "I don't know and I don't care. Once he's in the ground, our lives can return to normal, if that's even possible."

"I'm sorry to have brought his name into your house," Maile said, not knowing how else to apologize. She knew then how disrespectful it had been. She collected her bag, ready to leave.

The elderly woman returned with a message for the hostess.

"My mother wishes to treat your feet."

"My feet?"

"They are bothering you?"

"Well, yes, but…"

"Our home doubles as her clinic. She's an acupuncturist, and would like to give you a treatment."

"I'm not really prepared to pay…"

"She's offering it free. You came here asking about her granddaughter. My mother has always been quite fond of Laurie, even if the rest of us have mostly given up on her. If you have the time, she already has the room waiting for you."

When Maile was pulled from her sofa, she could barely resist.

"It's okay. It's safe. She has a license."

Maile was expecting a spa-type of room, but was led into a simple room not much bigger than a bedroom closet. A small fan perched on a stool whirred in one corner, and the only light was a ceiling lamp. A long bench with a thin pad and sheet sat against one wall.

Once she was stretched along the length of the bench, Maile's skirt was pushed up to expose her legs. Without a word, the granny began puncturing her skin with needles.

"You could give me a little warning before doing that," she muttered into her flat pillow.

One by one, along both legs, needles were poked into skin, spun a few times, before more needles were inserted. She lost track of how many were put in. The only other time she'd had acupuncture had been in nursing school, mostly to write a report about alternative therapies that might adjunct western care. As the woman continued to spin and wiggle needles, Maile could feel her feet getting warm, her circulation improving. A sense of relief came over her, and she was almost asleep when she felt needles being taken out again. When she was helped up to a sitting position, her head spun for a moment. Before that settled, the woman stuck a small slip of paper in her hand.

Going back through the house to the front door, the tea set had been taken away, and the little girl was quiet. The elderly woman said something in Chinese as she watched Maile put her shoes on again, and held the door for when she left. Maile gave her a quick wave goodbye. Walking to the sidewalk, she found her feet fit in her shoes properly again.

"What was that all about?"

Faced with the decision of going home to her place, going to her mother's house for a meal, or going Christmas shopping at the mall, she decided against all of them and got something to drink at a neighborhood coffee shop that had been there since her high school days. Taking a seat at a window counter, she got out the slip of paper from the acupuncturist. Figuring it was a bill that needed to be paid, she unfolded it.

My grandmother wants you to send my sister home.

A phone number followed that message. It had been written by the young man, apparently Laurie's brother, before being handed off to the grandmother to give to Maile.

"Interesting. Passing secret notes in the Long house." She made the call, wondering what new mystery would be opened, or if a secret would finally be shared. "Thanks for the note. Why didn't you just talk to me at your house?"

"Laurie's a sore subject around here. The rest of us are trying to move on, but Granny keeps her alive. She wanted me to give you that note."

"That's fine, but it doesn't tell me anything about where I can find Laurie? I was just at a rehab center near the pali, and they tried telling me that a patient there was Laurie, but she didn't look familiar to me."

"Forget about her. You'll find what you're looking for this evening at the Kapalama Palms Community Center."

The call ended abruptly.

"Find what I'm looking for? Why do I get the idea the Longs are a little weird?"

Maile had to find the place on an internet map on her phone. It wasn't far from the same bus line she'd taken that morning. Catching a bus, she retraced her earlier steps.

Her feet and legs felt spirited as she walked from the bus stop to the community center. It was an older part of Honolulu, with small commercial areas mixed with residences. Houses were small with 'established landscaping', and businesses were family owned. There was a Hawaiian diner she and her mother liked going to near there occasionally, and Maile made the plan to stop in after looking for Laurie. That would relieve some of the disappointment if this trek turned out to be another wild goose chase like all the others that day.

When she got there, she discovered a wedding reception was being held. Having no idea of who got married that day, and not having an invitation, she went around to the kitchen and service side of the building. Standing near the doorway watching for Laurie in the kitchen, she wasn't one of the half dozen women preparing meals on plates.

"Are you one of the waitresses?" a woman barked at her. "You're supposed to be wearing a black skirt and a white blouse."

"Sorry, I'm looking for Laurie Long."

"Who? I don't have any waitresses with that name."

Maile gave it some thought. "Honey?"

"Or, her. You're with the police?"

"No."

"She's taking care of tables three, five, and seven. Go sit. She'll bring you something."

"I'm not an invited guest," Maile tried explaining to the busy woman.

"Half those people in there aren't and I'm supposed to find a way of feeding them all. Go sit anyway. Honey will bring you a plate."

Going back to the front entrance, Maile mixed in with several others that were dressed as though they had attended a wedding. Scanning the large dining hall decorated with flowers and cheerful garlands, she found a place at one of Laurie's tables to sit.

"Yeah, good. Crashing a wedding reception," she mumbled to herself. She was mostly ignored by the others at the large table, who were sharing stories about the newly married couple. When a waitress brought two plates to be served, Maile had to look twice at her. Since the last time she'd seen her, Laurie—or maybe Honey—had lost weight and her hair was black again. Her makeup was still a little heavy for Maile's tastes, but was a lot less dramatic than what she remembered seeing on her. It didn't ease her confusion, though.

She came over to where Maile waited. "Beef or chicken?"

"Maybe just something to drink."

"Someone else is bringing champagne." Laurie looked at Maile a little closer. Now with recognition in her face, her eyes squinted and jaw muscles worked overtime. "Beef…or chicken?"

"Beef, I guess. Actually, I need to talk to you about something."

A waiter carrying a full tray of glasses stopped at the table, allowing another waitress to deliver glasses of champagne to each guest.

"Please, enjoy you drink," Laurie said with fake courtesy, before leaving in a hurry. Ten minutes later, she delivered a meal to Maile. When she left, a slip of paper was beneath the plate, a corner of it showing. Maile slipped it out from its hiding place.

"More secret messages from the Longs," she mumbled. "I'm not entirely sure if I'm supposed to call this one Laurie or Honey."

She looked at the note while hiding it in her lap.

I get a break once everyone is served.

Unsure if a meeting had been scheduled, Maile began on her meal. All she could guess was that it was a Salisbury steak, possibly the smallest she'd ever had, but it was free and she was an uninvited guest, so she couldn't complain. By the time she was done with it, she wanted to get a business card, just so she could eliminate them if she ever needed a caterer in the future. When the guests at the table were mostly finished and began chatting again, Maile looked for Laurie. She saw her at the far end of the room near the exit, vigorously waving a hand for her to join her.

Maile finished the champagne in one swallow. Not knowing exactly what to do with her plate, she left it behind. When they met at the door, Laurie took her by the arm and went outside.

Standing near the parking lot, Laurie lit a cigarette. "Why are you here?"

"I need to talk to you about Oscar."

"Who sent you? The cops?"

"No one sent me."

"How'd you find me, then?"

Maile found the slip of paper that she got from Laurie's grandmother and handed it over.

"That's my brother's writing. You were at their house?"

"For a few minutes."

Laurie dropped the half-smoked cigarette and stubbed it out with the toe of her shoe. "Look, I'm done with Swenberg, okay? You and the cops need to figure that out and leave people alone."

"So, you're still going by Honey or by Laurie again?" Maile asked.

"Laurie. Try to keep up, okay?"

"Don't say that. Look, there's no trouble, at least not for you. I only need to find Oscar."

"I'm starting over in life and everything is going okay. Why can't the social workers understand that?"

“I’m glad things are going well for you. The only reason I’ve come to you is to find out if you know where I can find Oscar.”

Laurie lit another cigarette, her hands shaking. “This isn’t easy starting over, you know?”

“I know, and I’m glad you are.” Maile wondered if she was making any headway in her simple quest at prying information out of Laurie. “Do you have a good place to live?”

“Not as nice as Hawaii Kai.”

“Not many places are. Are you able to help me or not?”

“What’s in it for me?” Laurie asked.

Maile had an idea. “You like being a waitress?”

“I get paid.”

“Is it full-time?”

“Weekend gigs, and Friday evenings sometimes. Why? You know of something better?”

Maile was having second thoughts about her idea. “Maybe. How are you with computers?”

“I know the basic operations. I thought you were a nurse? Why are you asking about computers?”

“I have a tour company and need someone to work in the office doing sales and phone work. Is that something you’re able to do?”

After one last drag, Laurie dropped the second cigarette and stubbed it out. “I sold my body in pornos. I think I can sell Waikiki to tourists."

Maile gave her a business card for Manoa Tours. “If you want a real job and a steady paycheck, be there tomorrow morning.”

"Thanks." Laurie tucked the card away. "Oscar left the hospital."

"Most of Honolulu already knows that. Did you help him?"

"No. I told you I want nothing to do with that guy. Why should I help him?"

"I don't know. We're just trying to figure out where he went."

Laurie looked at her watch. "He's staying with a lady in a house near Punchbowl, on Kamamalu Avenue."

"That's why you don't want to talk about him? Because he's living with someone else?"

"No, duh."

"Be careful. If you get that job tomorrow, I'm the one that would be signing your paycheck."

"Sorry."

Maile asked the question everyone in Honolulu needed to find a specific address. "How will I know the place?"

"You'll know it when you see it. The lady he's shacked up with is the neighborhood cat lady."

"Thanks."

"Nainai gave you acupuncture, didn't she?" Laurie asked.

"Your grandmother? Yes. How'd you know?"

"I can see it in your color. You're all flushed. She needles everyone. Mother calls it a business, but Nainai doesn't make much money at it."

"She should charge. She's good at it. Should I send her a check?"

“Forget it. I doubt Nainai even has a bank account.” Laurie checked her watch again. “I need to get back to work. You’re serious about tomorrow?”

“Only if you’re serious about wanting the job. Better than carrying plates of food around with your thumb in the gravy.”

Chapter Eight

Maile had more walking to do if she wanted to find the house where Oscar Swenberg was living. Two or three streets circled the famous cinder cone crater known as Punchbowl, the home of Hawaii's National Cemetery of the Pacific. She took a bus to as close as she could before getting out and beginning the spiral walk through a residential neighborhood. As she passed houses, she watched for congregations of cats in the yard. It wasn't until she got to the end of the street that a cat strolled out to meet her.

She rubbed behind the cat's ears. "Are you the official greeter?"

After a moment, two more cats came out and circled around her legs, brushing up against her, seeking affection. Maile looked up at the house. Not much could be seen through clean windows with drawn curtains. The lawn was neatly mown and edged along the sides, tidy hedges marked lot lines, paint on the walls was drab but new, and the front walk to the door had recently been swept. The car in the small carport was a late model luxury sedan that didn't fit the modest neighborhood. That's where two more cats were lounging in the shade.

The scene reminded Maile of what Detective Ota had said about Oscar's hospital room, how it had been left in a neat and tidy condition when he quietly left late one night.

"Sometimes people expose their own secrets without meaning to."

Maile went to the front door anyway. Giving it a half-hearted knock, someone came to the door, but didn't open it.

"Yes?"

There was nothing else to do but to say it. "I'm looking for Oscar Swenberg."

"He's not here."

"I need to talk to him."

"Who are you?"

"A friend…of Honey." Wondering if that was enough, Maile added, "I have something for him."

The door eased open, the security chain remaining in place. "I told you, he's not here."

"Honey just told me an hour ago that he is," Maile insisted. She tried seeing past the woman into the house. What she could see mimicked the exterior, of being clean and organized.

"He was for a while, but he left."

"To?"

"He needed more than what I could give him."

Maile was tired of the game. Plus, her feet were beginning to throb again. When she stuck her foot in the door to block it from slamming shut, she pushed back. "That doesn't answer my question."

"You're a bigger pain in the neck than the police."

"I'll take that as a compliment. Where's Oscar?"

"He's in a group home for people just like him."

"Which tells me nothing."

"You look smart. Figure it out for yourself." The woman slammed the door against Maile's foot. "Tell him Joey says hi."

Further from finding Oscar Swenberg than she had been at the beginning of the day, Maile went home. Picking off Band-Aids and rubbing her feet, she thought of Brock. She'd forgotten all about how he'd nearly galloped out of her apartment that morning, choosing to lie about meeting Detective Ota rather than go to breakfast with her. It had turned out to be a grim day.

***

In the morning, Maile was up before her alarm. When she heard footsteps out in the hallway, she peeked out to see Rosamie waving to her husband as he left for work. She watched as Rosamie came across the hall to knock on her door.

"Hi, Maile! Like some breakfast with me and the kids?"

"You know what? I wish I could, but I have to be in the office in a few minutes."

"Oh, yeah, new job. No more time to talk in the mornings?"

"On weekends."

"We're moving this weekend."

With a new disappointment in mind, Maile had to go. If nothing else, she needed to be at the office before her two new employees got there. If they even showed up. She wanted to spend some time chatting with her friend, but not about bad news. "I really have to go. Maybe tomorrow?"

As soon as she was out on the sidewalk for the walk to the office, her phone rang with a call from her mother.

"Legs okay?"

"Stiff, but okay."

"Left and right?"

"Yep, both of them are okay. Is that why you called, Mom, to ask about my legs?"

"To remind you about special service at church on Christmas Eve."

"I almost forgot." Maile rubbed her forehead. "Still two weeks away. What's so special about it?"

"You'd know if you came to church more often. Barely stayed long enough yesterday to say hi to Kelani."

"She sees me often enough. What was so important about yesterday?" Maile asked.

"Hasn't seen you perform hula in years. Still know how?"

"Yes, Mom, my soul is still Hawaiian. How is that so important to Auntie all of a sudden?"

"She's organizing a few things and wants you to perform hula after the Christmas Eve service. We all do. It doesn't have to be much, just a couple minutes is okay."

"How many people are going to watch me stumble through a poorly-rehearsed hula?"

"The usual group, maybe a few more. Maybe a little surprise for you."

"Not in the mood for surprises. What are you planning? Because I already had too much of a going away party the other day."

"Nothing like that. Maybe a little like that, but different. Just a special day. Want to make sure you're there for it."

Maile thought of her plans to spend the afternoon with Rosamie and her family in their new house on Christmas Eve. "I already have plans."

"A date with Brock?"

"I wish. Just spending the afternoon with a family."

"This is more important than that."

"Yes, I know. I haven't been coming to church as much as I should. But Reverend never has a special service on Christmas Eve. What's so special this year?"

"You'll know when you get there."

"Now you're the one keeping secrets from me!" Maile said, rounding the corner to her office.

"Not so nice, is it? Special service at three o'clock. Be there early." With that, Kealoha ended the call.

When Maile got to the Manoa Tours office, she didn't get a sense of ownership, but more of dread that something was going to go wrong that day. She'd been owner of the small company all along, although she hadn't known it. The only part of the business she'd paid attention to was her role in giving tours. Now, she was responsible for every aspect of running the company. That meant checking the books that had been kept by her predecessor, her brother-in-law, Thomas. The first task of the day was to hire a tour guide, and that was Susan Ota.

Susan was already there waiting at a desk in the office, with Lopaka seated at another desk, keeping an eye on her. The company's only full-time guide, Christy, was also there with her driver Danny, working on that day's itinerary. One person wasn't there, that being Laurie Long.

"I guess a meeting is in order," Maile told the others. She made a brief explanation about how Thomas would no longer return, and that she was the official owner of the place. She also told them of her plans to hire someone to run the office. "Unless one of you wants to?"

They each got busy shuffling papers or clicking on keyboards attached to computers that weren't turned on.

"Anyway, Christy and Danny have a day full of tours to give, and I'm hoping Susan agrees to work with us and take a group out this afternoon. I was expecting someone named Laurie to show up this morning to help with sales. Was she in?"

They all shrugged. With that, Christy and Danny went off to collect their first group in Waikiki, Lopaka went out to attend to his van, and Maile had Susan bring a chair to sit with her at the desk Thomas had used for years.

"Your Japanese language skills sounded really good when I heard you talking at the potluck the other day," Maile said to Susan. "Would you be able to lead a tour in Japanese?"

"I think so. I spent the weekend studying vocabulary and refreshing my memory of grammar."

"Sounds like you worked hard."

"My dad made me. But I was going to study anyway. Honest!"

"I believe you." Now came the hard part in the hiring process. Maile had never been a boss of anything before, never responsible for hiring or firing anyone. "Okay, I have your application for employment here. Thanks for coming in early and filling it out. You worked at a department store a few years ago. Was that in high school?"

"I'd already quit school by then."

"You haven't finished high school yet?"

Susan eased back in her chair. "Wasn't the best student."

"Any other jobs?"

"Just the profession you already know about."

"Thanks for reminding me. Maybe it's best if we both forget about that experience. That's why you're here, to start fresh, right?"

"If that Lopaka guy lets me."

"Don't worry about him. He's very loyal to the company and wants the best for it. If we go under, he needs to find another job, which he doesn't want to do."

"He's very loyal to you, Maile. Or should I call you Miss Spencer?"

"I'd prefer Maile. And yes, we're loyal to each other. We've known each other for a long time, and we worked well together when I was a guide. I'm hoping the two of you can carry on that tradition, of getting along and having a good time on the tours. The guests respond to that, and happy guests are generous guests when it comes time to hand over tips at the end of a tour. Remember that."

They talked about the types of tours Susan would take guests on, and how it had helped Maile to brush up on places in her spare time.

"Your tour today is to take a small group of Japanese housewives to the National Cemetery, Pearl Harbor, with a quick stop at the Royal Mausoleum. Have you been to any of those places lately?"

"Field trips as a kid."

"You'll need to be more familiar than that, but you have time to read about them before the tour starts. Lopaka will help you, making sure you get to the right place at the right time. These ladies will probably already know a lot about the cemetery and Pearl Harbor, and your visit to the mausoleum isn't a big deal. Just point at the tombs, interpret the signs, and that's good enough. But most important…"

"Don't talk to them like a hooker?" Susan said.

"Well, yes. But even more important than that is to always be polite to guests. If these ladies expect you to bow, do it. Please and thank you go a long way in the hospitality trade."

"Act like an airline attendant?"

"Basically. Remember, they're paying us a lot of money to take them places they can get to on their own. Show them a good time." Maile felt compelled to add, "Without acting like a hooker."

"I'm hired?" Susan asked, sitting up straight.

"Yes." They discussed the pay and the minimal benefits, which was more than what Maile got when she worked as a guide. "You have about three hours to read about your destinations. You might want to bring up each site on your phone and bookmark them for later."

"I should go to the library," Susan said.

"For?"

"To read some books about these places."

Maile pointed at a computer. "Just read online about them."

"Not really sure…I'm not so good with computers."

"You've never used one?"

"Never needed one with my old profess…what I did before."

Maile took her to a computer. "It's not much different from using data on your phone, only bigger and faster."

She watched Susan navigate the keyboard one finger tap at a time, looking more like a schoolgirl than a tour guide. Maile checked out her outfit again, modest in Susan's world, but good enough for being a guide. Satisfied Susan was under control, Maile went out to find Lopaka checking under the van's hood.

"You hired Susan?" he asked, slamming the hood down.

"Yeah. Are you going to be able to deal with her?"

He began checking air pressure in tires. "I don't like the idea of somebody like her working for you."

"She's working for Manoa Tours. Otherwise, she's made all sorts of promises about being prepared for tours, and that she's turning over a new leaf in life."

"But do you trust her?"

"We're on a small island in the middle of an ocean. If she beats you up and steals the van, she won't get far."

Lopaka laughed. "Okay. If she's good enough for you, she's good enough for me."

"What's the deal between you and her father, anyway?"

"Detective Ota? You'd get a better answer from him about that than from me."

"That's what he always says," Maile said, going back to the office. There, she set about searching files, trying to make sense of the spreadsheets that Thomas had used. He'd spent almost no money on advertising, but at least the books balanced, and the company had been consistently in the black. Manoa Tours wouldn't be listed on the stock exchange any time soon, but it was a small business that showed a profit, which gave Maile no reason to shut it down. "Doesn't mean I wouldn't sell it to the highest bidder, though."

Maile barely noticed when Lopaka and Susan left for their tour. She was alone in the quiet office then, still studying the bookkeeping that Thomas had left her, when her phone rang. The number was familiar but she couldn't place it.

"Maile, this is Brian, Brock's brother."

"Oh, yes, hi. If you're looking for him, you'll have to call his phone directly."

"I'm looking for you. I just got through with my appointment with that eye doctor your set me up with."

With the way he put it, Maile wondered if there had been trouble. "How'd it go?"

"Better than planned. Doctor Nakamoto is nice."

"Good. What did she say about your eyes?"

"Really nice office. Nothing like the VA clinics I've been to."

"I'm not familiar with them. Did she do an exam?" Maile asked, still trying to focus on the computer spreadsheet while listening to Brian.

"The receptionist, the office assistant, all first rate."

"What about the exam?"

"She did one. I thought I'd have to come back another time for that."

Maile sighed. "What did she find with the exam?"

"That I'm mostly blind in both eyes because of the scar tissue."

"You already knew that, didn't you?" she asked.

"Yes, but she said she can do something about it with surgery."

"That's great news!"

"My vision might not be perfect afterward, and I might have to wear glasses. Knowing me, I'll probably end up with those birth control glasses they give people in the military. Have you ever seen those?"

"Maybe I have. But getting back to the exam, what did she say she can do?" Maile asked.

"A keratoplasty," he said slowly, before spelling it. "You know what that is?"

"I'm not an eye expert, but I think that's when they remove diseased or damaged natural cornea and replace it with donor cornea. All those eye surgeries get pretty complicated."

"What do they mean by donor?"

"Well, when someone dies, they can donate organs for transplant."

"They can do that with eyes, also?"

"With the corneas. It's being done much more often lately. Sometimes that's all someone donates, is their corneas."

"It comes from a dead guy?"

"That's how they get organs for transplantation, yes."

"And it works?" he asked.

Maile closed one spreadsheet and opened another. "Apparently, or they wouldn't keep doing it."

"Why didn't the VA doctors ever tell me about this?"

"I don't know why. I've heard the VA operates on a tight budget. Maybe it's too expensive?"

"Should I have Doctor Nakamoto do my surgery?" he asked.

"If she thinks it'll help restore your vision, then yes. I know she's right out of training, and that often scares people away, but what I read about her the other day is that she trained at a top notch program." She wondered if she should, and then added, "I'd trust her."

"What about getting a second opinion?"

"She is your second opinion, Brian. The VA made it sound hopeless, and she's hopeful. I'd go with her, even if it's expensive."

"I have some money saved up for a down payment on a house. Just as good to spend it on surgery, I guess."

"Look at it as an investment. If you got good eyesight back, you could get a better job than doing your blogging and novel writing."

He chuckled. "Sounds like you're trying to turn me into a responsible citizen!"

"That's today's theme." She told him about taking over the helm of her little company, and already hiring a new employee with a questionable past. "When would she do the surgery?"

"This week. She has time on Wednesday. Is that too soon?"

"Better sooner than later. Just think, you might have some of your vision by Christmas!"

Chapter Nine

Maile spent the afternoon paying overdue water and electric bills for the office, and paid the next month's rent early. She figured out payroll, and when she saw how much Christy was getting paid, she decided she wouldn't be getting a New Year's raise, while Danny and Lopaka would. With a hurry to the teriyaki place next door, she got a late lunch, and was just finishing that when Lopaka and Susan returned from their tour. Susan looked frazzled as she flopped into a chair, but Lopaka was smiling.

"Well? How'd it go?"

Lopaka gave Maile a secret thumbs-up to show his satisfaction before going out to clean the van.

"I don't know," Susan said. "My brain's all frazzled from pretending to speak Japanese all afternoon."

"Any complaints?"

"No. They were a little confused with what I was saying a few times. Maybe my Japanese isn't so good after all?"

"I'm sure it was fine. Did they have a good time?"

"I guess so." Susan dug into a pocket. "This is the tip money they gave us."

With a glance, Maile could tell the guests had been generous. "Lopaka gets half of that."

"I already gave him his half."

"You got that much for a four hour tour?"

Susan shrugged. "I get to keep this?"

"It's all yours. You earned it."

She counted it again. "What should I do with it?"

"I don't know what you should do with it, but if I were you, I'd put it in my bank account."

"I'll have to open one. What should I do with the money I earn?"

"What did you spend it on before?" Maile asked.

"Clothes, food, a place to stay with some of the other girls. Things are different now. I don't want to live like that anymore."

"Maybe you can find a place to stay other than your dad's house. You might want to find GED classes so you could go to college someday."

"Me? College?"

"You're too smart not to. And it would make your dad even more proud of you."

"I doubt he'll ever be proud of me," Susan said, shoving the cash in her pocket again.

Maile got her things together, ready to lock up for the day. "You'd be surprised."

***

For as much time as she'd spent looking through company records that day, Maile had spent at least as much time searching for long term housing that Oscar Swenberg might be living in. But with each passing day, she was less and less concerned with where he was on Planet Earth. More interesting than finding him was why Laurie hadn't shown up that day.

Once Lopaka left, Maile turned the lights off in the office and locked the door. With only a computer for company, she resumed her search for either Oscar or Laurie on the internet.

"Okay, nobody knows where Oscar is, and the idea that I might find him is pretty absurd. But I would like to know why Laurie didn't show up for work this morning. If I had a guide that spoke Chinese, or at least a salesperson, I could double the number of tours for as many Chinese tourists there are in Hawaii these days. This crummy little company could turn into something."

She dug through her bag for the business card she'd gotten the day before at the wedding reception for the catering company.

"Carrot Top Catering? Oh, I get it. The woman running the company was a redhead."

She looked at the card for a moment, trying to make a decision. Getting out the two secret notes that had been passed to her by Laurie and her family, she read those again. There had to be a clue in there. The first one was from Laurie's grandmother, something that had been written by her brother:

My grandmother wants you to send my sister home.

There was something fishy about the note. It was obvious the grandmother hadn't written it; she barely spoke any English, and probably wrote even less. It was either Laurie's brother or mother, and the mother seemed more interested in getting rid of Maile rather than helping her.

She read the other note, the small slip from Laurie herself:

I get a break once everyone is served.

That's when it dawned on her what was so strange about the two notes. She put them side by side for comparison.

"Well, now aren't you clever." Getting the two notes at separate times prevented Maile from noticing they were written by the same hand. It was obvious someone had tried to disguise one or both of them, but the way the Ts were crossed and how the trailing ends of Gs and Ys were so similar, it had to be the same person. "You were there when I stopped in for a visit yesterday, weren't you? You wrote and gave the note to your grandmother yourself. She never knew any better because she couldn't read what it said. You sneaky little…"

Drumming her fingers on the desk, she decided to call the caterer.

"Yes, hi. My name is Mary Spellman. I own a tour company and I have a job application here for someone named Laurie…Honey Long. It states she works for you. Is that correct?"

"I have a Honey that works occasionally as a waitress, but her last name isn't Long."

Maile had a pretty good idea of what was coming. "What is it?"

"I don't know. She only goes by Honey. You know, like those entertainers with no last name."

"If she has no last name, how do you pay her?"

"Cash at the end of a job. Some of the waitstaff prefer it that way."

"And she never mentioned any last name?"

"No, sorry. Who is this again?"

"Mary Stimson. Do you have her address handy? Or phone number?"

"That should be on her application."

"She has something listed here, but when I call, there's no answer. I'd like to call her for an interview. I'm not taking her away from you. I just need her during the week."

"You can have her and keep her," Carrot Top said.

"It sounds like you're not recommending her?"

"Not as a waitress. Half the times she took the wrong meals to the wrong patrons, and the other half of the time she had her thumb in the gravy."

"I noticed that. I mean, she wouldn't work for me as a waitress," Maile said.

"I have her number and address here for you. I got the idea things were temporary for her. Maybe she'll find a home with you."

Maile jotted down the address and phone number that Carrot Top provided. The address was different from the Long family home, only a short bus ride from the tour office. After thanking the caterer, she saved the phone number into her phone's memory.

Maile thought better of calling Laurie, that she wouldn't get far in knowing why she didn't show up that morning. She knew she'd have to be direct, and make a surprise visit on her if she expected reasonable answers. Instead of doing something impulsive, Maile locked up and left work to find Laurie all over again.

The address she got from Carrot Top was in Waikiki, in one of the few older residential neighborhoods that still existed. High-rise condos shared space with old apartments in the area, and Maile needed to walk up and down the street a couple of times before she found the right place. From seeing the outside, the building had to be one of the oldest in Waikiki, a two-story thing leftover from the 1950s.

She went to the door that was listed as Laurie's address and knocked. There was a strong scent of something burning, and it wasn't incense. After she knocked a second time more insistently, someone came to the door but didn't open it.

"Who is it?"

Maile wanted to say 'Dave'. "I'm looking for Honey."

"What for?"

"I need to talk to her. It's important."

The door opened a little and a blond haired, blue-eyed woman's face peeked out. "You a social worker?"

Maile's brow furrowed all on its own. "No. A friend of Honey. Is she here?"

"Not since this morning."

"Can I come in and see for myself? This is important."

The woman let Maile in. "Sure you're not a social worker?"

The pungent scent was even stronger, with a slight haze in the room. With a closer look at the girl, she was a bottle-blond, the same color surfers use. "Certain. Why do you ask that?"

"You look like a social worker."

"Thanks. I'm not. Honey lives here with you?"

"And some other girls. Is she in trouble?" Blondie asked.

"Not with me. Can I see her room?"

Blondie took Maile down a hall past two other rooms. The whole place had a wannabe hippie feel to it, with posters on hallway walls, and bead curtains in doorways. "She shared this room with Nan."

There was only one bed in the room, an unmade single bed. The rest of the room was crammed with old sticks of furniture and boxes of stuff. Someone was either just moving in or moving out. Maile lifted the flaps to a few to see what was inside.

"Are these boxes Honey's or Nan's?"

"Who cares? No one ever unpacks much stuff around here."

"They don't stay long?" Maile asked, looking through a box of clothing, trying to recognize something she'd seen Laurie wear.

"Nowhere to put the stuff. When they leave, most of it is left behind."

"You know when Honey's supposed to get home?" Maile asked.

"I'm not sure she's coming back."

"Oh, why?"

"Come with me," Blondie said. They went to the only bathroom in the apartment, where she got the trash bin to show Maile. "She did this before she left today."

Inside the basket were several packages, the kind of thing that would be found in any woman's bathroom wastebasket. There was also hair. Maile pulled some out for a look and dropped it back in again.

"She gave herself a haircut?"

"Cut her bangs. It looked pretty good by the time she was done." Blondie rummaged through the basket for a box. "She used this to put a few highlights in. I used the rest on my hair. How do I look?"

Maile gave her a glance. "Good. Super cool. She cut her hair and then streaked it?"

"Yeah. She had a little booklet that she was looking at."

Maile looked at the box of hair dye. "What kind of booklet? Hairstyles?"

“No, just a little thing. It had a picture of her inside. She said it was from a long time ago.”

“Was it green? And it had empty pages inside? Sort of official looking?”

Blondie snapped her fingers. “You know, I think you’re right.”

Maile had seen the same thing a few months before, another time when she was looking for Honey. Right then, she couldn’t remember the name that was inside. All she knew was that it had been a Spanish passport. “Was it a passport?”

“I guess.”

Maile dropped the box back into the basket and looked at strands of hair again, trying to guess what Laurie’s hair might look like now. “Did she take anything else with her?”

“She had a big bag like yours. Kinda full. Maybe she had some clothes in it? I don’t know.” Blondie led Maile back to the small living room, where there was a new haze in the air from another joint being smoked. “Hey, you wanna smoke for a while?”

“No. Thanks, though. My mind has had enough for today.”

Maile needed a meal, and even more, some help. Taking a chance as she walked away from the apartment, she dialed a number. When Brock answered, she sighed with relief.

“Busy?” she asked.

“Just got home from work. Brian told me the good news.”

"It's great news." Maile bit her lip, wondering if she should proceed. "Hey, I'm in Waikiki and I'm hungry. Can I buy you dinner?"

"You're buying for a change?"

"You make me sound like a cheapskate."

"You've always been on a tight budget."

"I've been living on a budget that didn't exist. I have a little money in the bank, so I may as well spend it. Are you hungry or not?"

They met at Denny's in Waikiki and immediately got a table.

"How was your first day as owner of Manoa Tours?" he asked after they ordered.

"I went, I saw, it conquered me."

"It'll get better."

"It'll get better for someone else. I'm thinking of selling it. I might be too busy to run it pretty soon, and don't want to try and deal with a company from a distance. I'm not cut out to be a businesswoman, anyway."

"Don't look at me. I don't have any money. I doubt I'd be any better at running a business than you will. That's Brian's deal. He got the management gene from our father."

"And you got your mother's looks?" she asked.

Brock cocked his head. "Feeling a little hostile?"

"Just trying my hand at stand-up comedy, something else I apparently suck at."

He finally smiled. "It was a good comeback. I just didn't expect it from you."

Their meals came and Maile watched as Brock heavily salted his T-bone steak. "That much salt isn't good for you."

He stopped shaking salt and looked up from his plate.

"What's your blood pressure?" she asked.

"Not as good as yours, but it's good enough to pass a police department physical. Is that why you asked me to dinner? To give me a physical exam?"

"Maybe." Maybe she'd inhaled a little too much second hand pot at Blondie's place, but Maile was feeling silly and gave in to the urge to tease Brock. "A little later I'll have you turn your head and cough."

"You had your chance the other night but dozed off, remember? Still feeling a little hurt about that."

"Poor baby."

"Do you harass all of your dinner dates?" he asked.

"It's been so long since I had one, I don't remember. I do have a couple of questions. First, I want to know why you made a jailbreak from my apartment yesterday morning?"

"I didn't make a jailbreak."

"You blasted out of there like you were trying to avoid a life sentence. And don't tell me a lie about having to meet with Detective Ota. I called him and he said he hadn't seen you all day."

"I had somewhere to go that couldn't wait."

"Something to do with Miss Wong?"

"Nothing to do with her," he said, cutting through his meat. "I just needed to help somebody move some stuff."

"Who?"

"Kind of personal, okay?"

"Laurie Long?"

"Who?" he asked.

"Honey Blond Swenberg."

"Why would I help her move?"

"I don't know. Was it another woman?"

"Yes, and a man. And that's all you need to know. What was your other question?"

Not wanting to pick a fight, Maile moved on. "Detective Ota asked me to look into Oscar Swenberg's case, of why he might've walked out of the hospital and where he went. But I'm completely lost."

"You don't have to, just because he asks."

"I know, but there's a reward."

"How much is it?" he asked. Brock whistled when she told him the amount. "That much just to find someone?"

"Someone worth a lot of money, and apparently doesn't want to be found."

"What have you done so far?"

"I decided to look up Honey…Laurie Long for help. I found her yesterday, only after a wild goose chase. She no longer lives at home with her family, but I was able to track her down to an apartment here in Waikiki. I just came from there."

"What did she have to say?"

"Another wild goose chase. She wasn't there. I did talk to her yesterday at a wedding I crashed, and…"

"You crashed a wedding? Whose?" he asked.

"I have no idea. But I talked to Laurie for a few minutes at the reception. She was the one who sent me on the wild goose chase to Punchbowl."

"The National Cemetery?"

Maile shook her head. The neighborhood just outside. The woman I talked to sent me away empty handed."

"I'm confused," Brock said. "I thought you just talked to Honey, or Laurie, whoever she is these days?"

"That's all a part of the fun of being on a wild goose chase, except I kinda tired of getting goose by both of them. All I want is to find Oscar and turn him over to Ota, for whatever reason he has for needing him."

"So, go back to Laurie and press for better info."

"That's what I did this afternoon, but it looks like she's skipped town."

"How do you know that?"

"Remember how I found Spanish passports for Oscar and her on his yacht at his house party that time? Well, she changed her appearance to look like the person in the passport. The people she was living with said they weren't expecting her to come back. Not that they were reliable."

"If she's traveling on a fake passport, TSA will pick her up at the airport."

"They sure looked legit to me. But I'm back to looking for Oscar. He's supposedly in a group rehab center, but those places keep patient identities close to their chests. Any idea of how I might be able to track him down?"

"Why is it so important that he gets found? Maybe he just wants to be left alone?"

"Money and closure would be my guess," she said. "Ota knows the real reason why, something he's not sharing with me."

"You don't have to help. You have your new business to mind. It might be time to forget about Oscar Swenberg and move on."

"I guess I've spent so much time on him and his brothers this last year or so, that I just want to get to the bottom of whatever his story is. Then I can let it go. I wouldn't mind getting that reward, too."

"Rewards are for bounty hunters, Maile. Don't start doing that stuff or you'll be asking for trouble."

"I've already had far more than my fair share of trouble with the Swenbergs. I just want to put it to rest." She shook her head. "There's something going on with that guy. Someone just doesn't walk away from the hospital for no good reason, and then promptly disappear. And why would Laurie walk away from all his money, from living in his house in Hawaii Kai?"

"Discovered she doesn't love him after all?" Brock offered.

"You saw that house, and the neighborhood. If he has half as much money as I think he does, I'd stick it out with him for longer than this, if I were Laurie. A young woman would really have to hate a guy to walk away from that life."

"Speaking from experience?" he asked.

"I stuck it out with Robbie for a year or two too long, and every dime I earned went into that stupid bar, while living in the cheapest condo Waikiki had to offer. So yeah, I'm not above sticking it out with a guy for a while if there was a decent gravy train."

"I'll have to keep that in mind," Brock said, working on his baked potato. "I wish I could help, but police files and investigations are privy to the police only."

"Does that mean Ota knows more than what he's telling me?"

"It means it's a fluid situation and that's all I can say." They finished their meals and ordered coffee. "Speaking of privy information, where are you going to work?"

"Still planning on going to the mainland for a while."

"Which state? It must be a big job to lure you from here. Tell me about it."

"It's a fluid situation and that's all I can say."

He smiled and nodded at her touché.

"What about us?" she finally risked asking.

"If you're leaving soon, not much can start, right?"

"I suppose. Is that why you left in such a hurry yesterday?"

"We already hashed that out." He smiled. "Tell you what? I don't have to be up early in the morning. Care to give me a second chance at over-staying my welcome?"

Chapter Ten

On Wednesday, both tour vans went out as planned, and Maile made a few follow-up thank you calls to previous guests. After placing several sales calls, she had other business to attend to. Brian was at the hospital that day for his eye surgery, and she wanted to be there when he came out. When she got to the hospital, she went upstairs to the Intensive Care Unit to see her old friend, Lei-lei, a nurse there.

"I've been hearing things about you, Mai."

"Good or bad?"

"All good, as always."

"Liars telling lies."

Lei-lei laughed. "Maybe so. I've heard you're leaving town for a while?"

"Where'd you hear that?"

"Honolulu is a big city, but a small town when it comes to the coconut cellular. Start talking."

"Nothing happens until after the new year." Maile told her friend about her plans, and where she was going. "You have to keep that quiet, even from my mom. I'm easing her into the idea of me leaving the island."

"You know, I never would've thought it, but you'll be perfect for that. Coming back someday?"

"Oh, yeah. Hawaii is home."

Lei-lei finished the dressing change on her patient. "Yeah, the islands are as much a part of our souls as poi is in our butts. Speaking of which, you won't be getting much poi where you're going."

"Probably not."

"Leaving Brock behind unprotected?"

"Oh, you know about him."

"Everybody does, Mai. Once your mother gets a hold of something like that, most of the island knows by the next afternoon."

Maile smiled. "Good old coconut cellular."

"And our church is the broadcast node!"

When Maile got to the surgical waiting area, she found Brock and Amelia sitting together. While he fidgeted, Amelia sat stoic, staring straight ahead with sightless eyes of her own.

"Have we heard anything?" she asked.

Amelia pushed a button on her watch to hear the time. "Not yet four hours."

"Sometimes these things take a little longer, and sometimes they go a little quicker. We just have to wait," Maile said.

"Funny how things work," Amelia said. "We ran a four hour marathon the other day, which amounted to nothing more than sore muscles and blistered toes. But in the same amount of time, Brian might get his sight back."

"He'll still have a long way to go, and might not have perfect vision." Maile looked at Brock to make a point. "We all need to be prepared for that."

Dr. Nakamoto came out then, still dressed in surgical scrubs. She'd just finished with Brian's surgery.

"Both sides went great. The donor graft was perfect, couldn't have been better. I also found damage to his lenses, so I put in intraocular lenses to replace those. It's pretty unusual, but I think he'll have very good eyesight."

"Does he need to wear bandages?" Brock asked.

"Just eye patches for a few days. I want him to come to my clinic on Friday so I can check the sutures."

The doctor went through the usual warnings and precautions on how to take care of his eyes for the next few days, and what to expect in the coming weeks and months.

Maile accompanied the group back to Brock's apartment in Kaimuki and made sure all three of them understood the post-operative instructions. Before leaving, she handed out one last stern warning to not mess with dressings or medications, or else they might have to start all over with more surgery with a new graft.

Brock walked her down the steps to the quiet sidewalk.

"What're you grinning about?" she asked him.

"Nothing. Just happy."

"I'm so glad he was able to have his surgery. It's super important that you guys follow the post-op stuff to the T."

"We will. But that's only half the reason I'm happy."

"He found a good surgeon. Doctor Nakamoto will take care of him," Maile said.

"Still not the reason," he said, maneuvering her around to a shady spot near the building.

When he leaned in with the beginnings of a pucker on his face, she put her hand on his chest. Without pressing too hard, she asked, "Feeling randy? Because your place is crowded and mine is too much of a dump to invite guests."

"Been there, done that, remember?"

"So romantic when it's put that way."

"I meant in your apartment."

"I know what you meant. What do you mean to get right now?"

"I'll take what I can get, even if it's on the sidewalk."

"Even my place is more romantic than this sidewalk."

"You just told me it wasn't."

"Are you going to kiss me or not?"

Once Maile's internal world stopped swirling after the kiss, and Brock had gone back upstairs, she set off down the sidewalk in search of a bus stop on Waialae Avenue, the main business street through Kaimuki. One thing she'd completely forgotten about was Reverend Ka'uhane's missing ukulele. When she passed by a pawnshop, she stopped to look at the things in the window. She didn't know much about the places, only that they took things in on loan, and if a buyer was willing to spend the money for something that might be junk, it was theirs.

She didn't see the ukulele in the window, but there were guitars and other musical instruments, so she went in.

"How can I help you, Ma'am?" the broker asked. Standing behind a glass case was a middle-aged man with the largest handlebar moustache Maile had ever seen. Being ebony black, its color didn't fit his white hair. "Looking to buy or sell some jewelry today?"

"No jewelry, just looking for a ukulele."

"Every year, it's the same thing. People see the Merrie Monarch hula competition on TV and come in to buy any ukulele we have. The girls want to learn to dance, and the parents want to learn to play the uke. Then six months later, they bring the instrument back again."

"I'm looking for one ukulele in particular." She found the image of the instrument on her phone and showed it to Mr. Moustache. "Has this one been in?"

He shook his head, barely glancing at the image. "I don't have any at all right now."

"Take a better look at this one. It was lost last Saturday. You haven't seen it at all?"

He looked at the image more carefully, stretching it larger to see details. "Nope, sorry. It looks cheap. I doubt I'd take it into my shop."

"It's not cheap, just a little old. There's a maker's label on the neck. Is that a good brand?"

He enlarged the image even more. "Ukulele of Makaha. That's a good brand. I didn't see that. Hold one just a minute. I wasn't here over the weekend. Maybe my partner took it in?"

He got out an old-fashioned handwritten ledger and flipped through a few pages while Maile watched. Dozens of items had come and gone, some for loans, others sold. After checking the times and dates for the weekend, he slammed the ledger shut again.

"Sorry."

"What other shops would you suggest I check?"

"Like I said, it's a little too plain for a pawnshop, even with that label from a good uke maker. If I were you, I'd check at musical instrument stores."

"Not really familiar with those," she said.

"The biggest one that I know of is on King Street near McCully. I know they have a lot of stringed instruments, and take in used things from time to time. Whether or not they'd have your uke, I don't know."

"Okay, thanks." Just as Maile was about to leave the shop, she stopped. "By the way, they're called ukulele, not ukes."

It was a simple fifteen-minute bus ride to get to McCully street, not far from the office for Manoa Tours. She decided to visit the music store before heading back to work. Inside, musical instruments were positioned on shelves, some hung from the ceiling, while the expensive brass ones were in glass cases. One entire wall was dedicated to guitars and ukulele. Rock music played on a sound system, and a trumpet lesson was being given somewhere in a room not quite sound proof enough. While a shaggy wannabe rock star milled around the guitars, a man greeted Maile as she scanned the room.

"Are you the gal looking for one specific ukulele?" he asked. While the kid in there was the up and coming star, the clerk looked like the real thing, only a few decades late.

"How'd you know that?"

"I'm Larry. Just got a call from Pete, down at Pete's Pawn on Waialae. He said to expect you."

"Which means I'm being taken for a ride if you have it?"

"Maybe at some other places, but not here. He said you have a picture of something?"

Maile displayed the picture of Reverend Ka'uhane's instrument. Larry moved the image around so he could see the maker's name on the neck, before scrolling around a little more. "That looks like an authentic Makaha brand ukulele. Was it yours?"

She shook her head. "The minister at our church. He played it at a picnic on Saturday, and it disappeared sometime during the day. He's not even sure where he set it down. We all looked everywhere for it."

"Sorry to hear that, but I don't have it."

"Any idea who might? Or do I just need to keep looking at pawnshops and music stores?"

"I'll tell you something. Those guys at pawnshops don't know nothing when it comes to handmade musical instruments. Everybody looks for the big names. These old ukulele made from koa wood have beautiful tone, as long as they get played on a regular basis. People who know instruments know these smaller, handmade things are fantastic, both as playing instruments, and as collector items."

"Does that mean it's not junk?"

"If it's a true Makaha ukulele, and in good condition, it's not even close to being junk. But people try to fake the labels occasionally on junk, to pass it off as something good."

"I doubt our Reverend would do something like that," she said.

"He could've been the victim."

"That doesn't get me any closer to finding it."

Larry gave her a business card. "Send the image to me. I can post a picture of it on our bulletin board. Maybe somebody will see it around and let me know." He pointed at a bulletin board with a dozen pictures of missing instruments pinned to it.

"People really do steal instruments?" she asked, after sending the image.

"Keeps the pawnshops open, if they can come up with a good story of how they got it. Someone has to prove ownership before they can do business at a pawnshop."

"Does that mean Reverend Ka'uhane's ukulele is expensive?"

"If it shows up in an honest shop, and the seller can pass themselves off as the legitimate owner, yes, it would be expensive at resale. Most places would take it on consignment. But a legit shop owner would question how someone came to own an older Makaha, and also why they were selling it."

That was demoralizing. "I see. Thanks."

"I doubt someone will try to sell it. I bet it's going into a collection. It's very nice of you to help look for it, though."

"Are you trying to politely hint that I'm wasting my time looking for it?" she asked.

"Pretty much, yes."

"Well, just in case it does show up, you have my number," she said, before leaving his shop.

It was mid-afternoon by the time she got back to Manoa Tours, and Maile barely had the energy for the second half of her day. On the one hand, she'd been able to share in Brian's good news about his operation; on the other hand, she'd been advised to forget about ever finding Reverend Ka'uhane's favored ukulele. She made a few half-hearted sales calls, before giving up. Once both tour teams had returned from tours and gone home,

Maile shut down the office computers and turned off the lights for the day.

Instead of going home, she needed something to cheer her up. With Ala Moana Mall only a few blocks away, she walked there just as the sun was setting. Her legs were still stiff, but at least they were recovering from the marathon a few days before. Hitting some familiar shops for Christmas shopping, she got a few things for her mother, brother, and Lopaka. It was the second year in a row that she wasted no money on shopping for Robbie, which meant she could afford a trip to the food court while her gifts were being professionally wrapped.

"I wonder where that jerk is now?" she asked herself, digging into her meal. Taking the risk she was interrupting a stakeout, or maybe even an early dinner with his daughter, she called Detective Ota.

"Whatever happened with Robbie and Thomas?" she asked.

"Since Thomas broke no laws that we could discover, he cut him loose. Robbie is a different story."

"Is he going to jail? Because if he is, that would be an early Christmas gift for me."

"Probably not."

"What? Why not?"

"He's been charged with seven counts of mostly junk crimes. Even if the DA brings him to court, I doubt a judge would give him time, other than time already served. He might get a fine, which would be deferred until he has some money. Unless you want to pay it for him?"

"Not hardly. I thought the charges against him were pretty serious?"

"His lawyer was able to get most of them reduced."

"I wish I'd had a good lawyer when I was divorcing his mangy…sorry."

Ota chuckled. "For your information, you know his lawyer."

"Not David Melendez, is it?"

"You really think he'd defend your ex? Your first lawyer, Emily is defending her. Didn't you have some sort nickname for her?"

"Budget lawyer. That might be changing to another B-word, though. How'd Robbie find her? Lazy Lawyers 'r Us?"

"I get the idea they might've known each other for a while," he said.

"Don't tell me…"

"Somehow their paths crossed during your divorce from him."

"That weasel."

"You can't think of anything stronger to call him?"

"I was thinking of her. But what's it mean if she gets him off? He just goes back to work looking for another sap like me?"

"For some of those guys that originally come from the mainland, the judge gives them a choice. They can agree to go back to the mainland forever and the judge drops all charges, or if they insist of sticking around, they get community service, and a fine to pay. Which would Robbie take?"

"Whatever requires the least work and has the largest breasts. I'd be glad to pay for his one-way ticket to anywhere else. That right there would be a Christmas gift to both of us."

"Put it on your Santa list. Maybe it'll show up under the tree."

"Any news on Swenberg or Laurie Long?" she asked.

"Nothing on Swenberg. A few things aren't adding up right with Laurie, though."

"Such as?"

"There's almost too many of her. I'm beginning to think there are two Laurie Longs in Honolulu, both the same age, and both having gone to Central High School."

"That's where I went to school. I was a year older than the Laurie that took over as cheerleader when I graduated. I don't remember any other Longs there at the time."

"You still have a yearbook? Take a look," he said.

"At my mom's house."

Her curiosity getting the better of her, Maile got her wrapped gifts and took the bus to her mother's cottage in Manoa Valley. A stringer of lights had been put along the front porch railing and around the front door, twinkling in the dark. No one was home, leaving most of the house in the dark. Going in, she found a tree had been bought and stood naked in one corner.

"That's just too sad to look at with nothing on it."

She had to dig through a shed to find the box of tree ornaments. Figuring Reverend Ka'uhane would want to help decorate the tree, she divvied up the ornaments so everybody got their fair share, some for him, some for her mother, some for Kenny, saving her favorites for herself. After hanging a few on branches here and there, she put the gifts she'd bought that afternoon beneath the lowest branches, pushing them back a little to keep inquisitive fingers away. There was still a week to go before Christmas, and many more gifts would need to be bought and wrapped. If this year was anything like years gone by, Maile was sure to get a sweater with a Christmas motif, Rudolph's head, Santa's face, or a cheerful snowman. She never had figured out why she needed a sweater in the tropics, but she never said a word, wearing the thing twice before shoving it in a drawer.

Before she left, she went out to see her pet cockatiel, King, in his large aviary. Since she needed to scrape his perches and the floor, she let him out to look for a meal of insects in the flower garden. After filling his bowls with fresh seed, she went out to the garden to get him.

"King! Come!"

Frustrated that he wasn't behaving after calling him several times, she got a flashlight and went in search of him. The first place she went was to a border of vines, a place usually thick with bugs.

"King!"

Maile made a full lap around the backyard of both the little cottage and of the Manoa House next door. When she heard some noise that only he could make, an odd pronunciation of her name, she shined the flashlight up into the tree branches. Waving it about for a moment, she found his white body on a branch.

"King! Come! I don't have all night!"

"Mai-ree! Mai-ree!"

Maile stamped her foot the way she would at the beginning of a hula. “King, come down here!”

King fluttered from one branch to another, Maile chasing him with her light. When the beam began to weaken, she gave it a rattle. That only made the light go dark. Peering into the dark, she couldn’t find him in the branches. When she heard her name one last time, and a long flutter of his wings, she knew he was gone.

The little bit of Christmas cheer she held in her heart flew away with him.

Chapter Eleven

Ever since childhood, Maile had secretly counted down the days before Christmas, eliminating them one by one as the holiday grew near. It was the one day of the year that was guaranteed to be a day off from everything else, to open gifts, read cards from nearly forgotten relatives, and eat until she was overflowing with turkey and gravy. She had a game she played, that eves of eves of eves were counted and eliminated as Christmas Day approached. This day was the eve of Christmas Eve, the 23rd. Considering no one booked any tours for the next day, Maile only needed to wait for Lopaka and Susan to get back from their tours before she could close up the office until after Christmas.

While she waited, she thought of King again, and where he might've gone this time, and if he was coming back. Maile was just drying her eyes and blowing her nose when a tour van parked outside. When Lopaka and Susan came in, they both looked tired.

"Tough tour?"

Lopaka said nothing as he flopped into a chair.

"Like, what's wrong with some of these people?" Susan griped.

"What happened?"

"We were at the Ulupo Heiau and one of them gets lost. Couldn't find the guy anywhere."

Maile looked at Lopaka for verification. He nodded.

"You didn't leave him over there, did you?"

"The…he walked down the street to get something to eat without telling anyone. We were all running around like idiots looking for him, at the heiau, at the park nearby, everywhere. Then the…he shows up all fat and happy looking. That's when we decided to give up and come back."

"Did you give out the little gifts?"

"Those were so cute! The guests loved them," Susan said. Lopaka nodded with agreement.

"Speaking of gifts, here's yours from Manoa Tours." Maile handed them both envelopes and small packages. "Don't spend it all in one place."

Lopaka tucked his envelope away and kept the unopened gift box in his hand.

"I get something?" Susan asked.

"Of course you do."

Susan gently held the gift and envelope as though they were from outer space. She looked back and forth between Maile and Lopaka for a second. "But I don't have something for you guys."

"Did you get something for your dad?" Lopaka asked.

"Yeah."

"Then you got something for every dad everywhere." He gave Maile a quick hug and tousled Susan's hair on his way out of the office.

"I feel bad," Susan said to Maile.

"Forget about it. You're just starting out and have only got one paycheck so far. You've been doing great, by the way. At least according to Lopaka."

Susan looked at the gifts in her hand again. "Still…"

"You know what you can do for me? Go see your mom tomorrow. Take her some flowers. Make your dad take you. I think that'd be nice."

"It's been forever since I've been there." Susan got her bag, ready to leave. "I'm really doing okay?"

"You're a much better tour guide than you were at your old job."

"Ha! You never saw me at work back then!" Susan's face changed suddenly to embarrassment, her cheeks turning pink. "Sorry. Sorta didn't really mean to say that. Hey, you look sorta sad."

Maile explained about losing King the day before, and how he'd flown away before. "I'm not so sure he's coming back this time."

"Oh, sorry. Maybe he'll surprise you and come back on Christmas?"

"I'm just hoping he found a better deal out there than he had with me," Maile said. "He was saying my name the way he used to a long time ago, but he hasn't spoken in years. I'm surprised he still knew how. Honestly, it felt like he was saying goodbye."

Susan turned for the door but stopped. She made a stutter step toward Maile, before taking a full step. Maile never saw it coming, but got the world's fastest hug from her past cellblock nemesis, now employee.

***

Maile still had a long errand to run before going home. That meant a long bus ride to Kapolei, home of golf courses, big box stores, military housing, and a famous resort. What she was looking for was a group home, the name and address given her by Detective Ota earlier that day. It was Oscar Swenberg's latest address, no more or less reliable than the half dozen others she'd been to in the last week or so. Getting off the bus, she decided this would be the last leg of the weird wild goose chase she'd been on, promising herself to give up on finding him or collecting the reward money.

From the outside, the place looked more like a nursing home than a group home. When she went it, it had that medicinal smell that most people disliked. The employees were dressed in flowery aloha wear, and she wasn't sure what types of employees they were, if they were therapists of some sort, or nurses. Asking for Oscar at the front desk, she was pointed down a hall.

"So, he's here?"

"Oh, yes. Has been for a few weeks. Who are you again?"

"A friend of his and his wife."

"Wife?" the woman asked. Maile finally noticed the nametag she wore, indicating she was a nurse named Joy.

"Honey." When there was no recognition to the nurse's face, Maile tried again. "Laurie?"

The nurse laughed. "How many wives does Oscar have?"

"Who knows? Just why is he in a nursing home? Are his injuries so bad that he needs to be here for a while?"

"Injuries? I think you might be mistaken." Joy took Maile to an office and closed the door. "This isn't a nursing home. We're a hospice."

"Oh. I didn't know. I was told this is a group home."

"Oscar has cancer. When he was first diagnosed, he apparently decided against any treatment, except palliative."

"I see. I'm sorry, maybe I shouldn't have come," Maile said quietly.

"I think he'd like to have the company. No one else comes to visit. And to answer the question you're afraid to ask, probably a week or two. He's gone downhill a lot in the last few days."

Leaving the office, Maile looked down the hall, trying to decide what to do. There was only one answer to that.

Oscar's room was halfway down the hall. He had a room to himself, decorated like a bedroom. When she went in, he was aiming the remote control at the TV, going from one channel to the next. She barely recognized him, for the weight he'd lost since she'd seen him last.

"Oscar?"

He looked at her. It took a moment before recognition set in. "You're Spencer. You've been to the house a couple of times."

"Yes, sir, that's right."

He turned off the TV. "No need for formalities. Pull up a chair."

"I'm sorry to just drop in like this. I hope you don't mind."

"You're a friendly face." They talked for a moment about the last time she was at his home a few months before, everyone there suffering trouble during a hurricane. "In a way, I've been expecting you."

"I've been looking for you for several weeks."

He coughed a few times. “For the reward money that I’ve heard about?”

“Maybe a little,” she said. “It became more of a quest.”

“I imagine you’re curious as to why I’m here?”

“I just heard you have cancer. I’m terribly sorry. Nobody else seems to know about it.”

He had a coughing spell and spit into a tissue. “Which is exactly what I want. I didn’t want a lot of fake friends coming around offering fake sympathy.”

“What about Honey?”

Oscar eased the back of his bed down a little. “Yes, what about her?”

“Has she been around to visit?”

“Not Honey, no.”

“I’m a little confused about something. There almost seems to be two of her,” Maile said.

“There are. I’ll explain in a moment.” He pressed the button on his pain control machine long and hard. Maile waited for the morphine to kick in, and hoped it wouldn’t put him to sleep before she got her answer. “You found Laurie in that rehab center near the pali, didn’t you?”

“Yes. Which Laurie is she?”

“The real one, the one you would’ve known in high school.”

“What happened to her? I mean…”

“Why is she breathing through a tube in her neck? Hollywood happened.” He had another coughing spell. “No, it wasn’t Hollywood. She survived that monstrosity, only to come home as a party girl. She took one look at me and decided she could do better. She didn't want to get divorced, mainly because of the gravy train she'd hitched her wagon to. Then the night came when the hospital called. She'd suffered a stroke while partying a little too hard. That was six months ago and she's been in that place ever since. If God is truly merciful, he'll take her as quickly as he takes me."

So, it turned out that the bright and energetic teenager that took her position as high school cheerleader a decade before was now in a vegetative state, her family waiting for her to pass. Life had been cruel to the girl, but not as cruel as she'd been to herself.

"I'm sorry to have brought all this up. This was a terrible idea to drop in and start asking questions about things that are none of my business," was all she could think to say.

"I need to tell someone besides my lawyers."

"Who's the other Laurie, or Honey, whatever her name is? The one I've come to know most recently?"

"A woman I met in Spain a while back. When Laurie ended up in that rehab place, I went a little nuts. Spain has always been one of my homes, so I went there for a while. When I met Maria, she was a dead ringer for Laurie, just a little bustier." More coughing. "That's her real name, Maria."

"I guess it had been so long since I'd seen Laurie, I didn't notice the difference. But Maria looks completely Chinese," Maile said, still as confused as ever.

"Maria is actually Chinese by descent, an orphan adopted by wealthy Spanish parents and raised to be Spanish. Along the way, her parents sent her to Chinese language tutors, and even sent her to live in China for a while."

"How…"

"Emotions got away from me and somehow I fell in love with my wife's doppelganger. How's that for sick?"

"Not sick at all," Maile muttered, not really believing it. "Does Laurie's family not know the difference between them?"

"Oh, they don't really care who I've spent the last few months with. All they know is that their daughter is sucking air through a plastic tube."

"Might be a better way of putting it than that. They really do miss their daughter."

"Believe it or not, so do I. Maria has been trouble from the word go. We hooked up there in Spain, even when she knew I had a wife here, one that looks just like her. She didn't care. She just wanted her piece of the pie. How sick is that?" He coughed through another round of chest upheavals. "Just so you know, and I really do want someone other than my shyster lawyer to know this, that Laurie will be inheriting my wealth, not Maria. Hopefully, it'll be enough to cover the expenses of her care for a long time to come."

"Did you know Honey…Maria was staying with the Long family?"

He looked startled at the question. "She found them?"

"Apparently. They're not real happy about it, either," Maile said.

"What a mess I've made for them," he said quietly. "I need to get my lawyer to get rid of her, once and for all."

Maile didn't like the sound of that, especially coming from someone with old ties to organized crime. "Maria might've already gone back to Spain."

"No, she hasn't."

"How do you know?" she asked.

"Maria was here this morning."

"But you told me she hasn't been in to see you?"

"I said Honey hasn't been to see me, but Maria has. Just like you said, she's turned back into Maria again." More coughing. "I told her to go to a priest for confession, but she just started in on telling me how she was done with being Honey, and wanted to start over with me."

"But…"

"Right. I had to explain that couldn't happen. But she thinks she's inheriting everything and is sticking around to collect it. I wish I could see her face when she finds out she's getting squat."

"Whatever. I don't know anything about those types of things." Maile noticed the boom box CD player on his bedside stand and got an idea. "Do you listen to music?"

"They had me listening to those stupid affirmation discs until I convinced them they were pointless. Now I just listen to whatever music disc someone shoves in there. Lately, it's all Christmas, as if I want to hear that stuff."

Maile got a small package from her bag, a gift meant for Reverend Ka'uhane, and handed it to Oscar. "Merry Christmas."

Oscar took the gift and smiled at the bright red wrapping and simple bow. "All the money a man could want, and I'm happy with this."

"It's not much, just ABBA songs played on the ukulele." Maile gathered her things and prepared to leave. "I met Joey the other day. She said to say hi."

"You probably want some sort of explanation about her," he said.

"Not really." She forced a smile to him. "I meant it when I said Merry Christmas."

While Maile waited for a bus to come for her, she called Detective Ota.

"Another dead end," she told him, remembering Oscar's last words to her, to please keep his secret.

"I'm giving up on him," Ota said. "Wherever he is, he can stay there till he dies, for all I care."

"Me, too."

"I heard from Susan. You gave her a gift?"

"It's not much."

"And a bonus?"

"I'm kind of a softy during the holidays, I guess," she said. "She deserves it, for as hard as she's been working. Hopefully, her dad is being nice to her for Christmas this year?"

"Not much choice. I think some of you is rubbing off on her. She demanded we get a tree this year, and that meant half an hour of me crawling around under the house looking for the box of ornaments."

"I thought you guys were Buddhist? You celebrate Christmas, too?"

"More for the fun than the religion," he said.

"She has something else for you to do tomorrow. She'll need to run an errand, and I want you to take her on it." With that, her phone chimed with another call. "Hello?"

"My name's Larry. I own the music store on McCully. Weren't you looking for a special Makaha ukulele a while back?"

"That's right. Have you heard about it?"

"Someone brought it into my shop earlier."

"You have it? May I buy it?" she asked. The depressing afternoon was beginning to brighten.

"I don't have it. Knowing it was possibly hot, I couldn't accept it."

"Oh."

"But I do know where you can find it, though."

"Maybe you should call the police?" Maile suggested.

"I did. Their excitement level was less than atmospheric."

Maile wondered what she could do. "I can't just go get it from somebody."

"For enough money you can."

"How much do they want for it?"

"Ten grand."

Maile gulped. She wasn't sure if the large deposit had been made in her bank account yet, nor could she convince herself a ukulele was worth that much, even if it had been Reverend Ka'uhane's favorite. "Seriously?"

"That thing isn't just any ukulele. It once belonged to Israel Kamakawiwo'ole. You've heard of him?"

"Bruddah Iz? Everyone in Hawaii has. That's why they want so much money for it? Just because it belonged to Israel?"

"That's the amount they were asking for in here, before I tossed them out, yes."

"Even if I had that kind of money, which I don't, I don't know how to find them," she said.

"Come into the shop. They filled out a pawn card before they left. You can have it. The cops aren't interested in it."

"Wait a minute. Are you from the music store or the pawnshop I visited?" she asked.

"Music store. Half the stuff you saw here has come in either on a pawn loan or consignment. But I won't consign anything that I suspect is stolen. Are you coming in or what? Because I need to close up pretty soon."

It took Maile only a few minutes on the bus to get to Larry's music store. He already had most of the lights in the store turned off and acted as though he was waiting impatiently for her. Barely saying two words to her, he slapped the pawn card for the ukulele on the counter. When she tried to take it, he kept his hand firmly planted on the slip.

He cleared his throat noticeably.

"Oh, yes, I figured there'd be something like this."

She tossed down the twenty-dollar bill she'd kept in her pocket, just for that reason. Once she had the card, Larry began turning off the last of his lights and walked Maile to the front door.

"Nice doing business with you, Miss. Come back again sometime."

She went back to the bus stop, and had to run to catch the next one that was heading toward Waikiki, the area with the address on the card. She realized that her legs were back to normal, and even her feet felt good, now that the blisters had dried up and healed. Finding a seat near the exit door in the crowded rush hour bus, she looked more closely at the address.

"Kalakaua Avenue," she muttered, trying to place the address. "Twenty-four, twenty-five, Kalakaua. That's near Duke's statue. For as many tours as I've given tours down there, I should know the addresses to those places by know."

Waiting patiently as the bus made every stop in Waikiki, she watched the address numbers as they went along. Once she was close to where she wanted to go, she got off and walked the last half block. She stopped dead in her tracks when she found the building.

"I am so stupid." She double-checked the address on the pawn card. "Unbelievably stupid. And I paid twenty bucks for this."

Just to punish herself, she walked a lap around the Waikiki Police Station, a small house-sized building adjacent to the famous beach. Duke Kahanamoku's bronze statue was only steps away, a popular stop on the 'Introduction to Waikiki' tours she gave. There was no shop, home, or other business, no ukuleles, no musical instruments of any kind, other than the man playing Christmas tunes on his harmonica for coins being tossed into a coconut shell.

While Maile cursed the stars while standing in the middle of the sidewalk, a meter maid parked her little vehicle. On her way into the station, she walked over to Maile.

"Miss, may I help you?"

Maile showed her the card. "I was given this address to find someone, but apparently I'm being pranked."

The parking enforcement officer took the card and looked. “That’s this address, but this is a pawn ticket. Where’d you get this?”

“At the music store on McCully.”

“I know that place. I just came from that part of town. Why’d he give you a pawn ticket?”

“I don’t know. He told me a lot of his stock is taken in through pawn loans.”

“I’m sorry, but he can’t do that. He needs a specific license to run a pawnshop, and his business is a music store. Nowhere on his sign or his advertising does it say anything about that place being a pawnshop.”

“Larry lied to me?” Maile asked.

“About being a pawn broker, yes.”

The meter maid called for a patrol officer to join them. While they waited, they watched sunbathers and surfers dash back and forth across the street, to find sunshine and waves, or a respite from both. When a patrol officer joined them, the meter maid explained the situation with the pawn ticket. The officer took the ticket for a closer look.

“This is just the stub,” he said. “They made a transaction with the broker, and whoever has this stub can go in and claim the item by repaying the loan debt. What was the item?”

“Should be a ukulele, but right now, I’m not exactly sure,” Maile said, taking the stub back. “Is there any way I can find out how much is owed on the debt?”

The officer shrugged his shoulders. “If they just hocked it, it wouldn’t be much because it hadn’t been there long. Just the amount of the loan, plus maybe twenty-five percent and some handling fees. Was it a nice instrument?"

"Not that I ever knew of, but I heard from a music store owner it was a fancy hand-made brand."

He took the card back for another look. "This card looks like it comes from Pete's Pawn, on Waialae. If you follow this street to Kapahulu, then follow that to…"

"I know how to get there," Maile said. "I've already been there. Pete was the one who sent me to Larry's music store on McCully. That's where I got this card."

"That doesn't make sense to me, Miss."

"Not to me, either. It makes more sense that someone's playing some stupid practical joke on me. First thing tomorrow morning, I'm going to give Larry a piece of my mind."

"Miss, if I were you, I'd go to Pete's pawnshop and give it to him. It seems to me he has more to do with this card than anyone else. I'd take someone with you, though."

"I know just the person to do that, too," she said, once she was alone. She called detective Ota, who answered on the second ring.

"Spending my spare time reconnecting with my daughter, remember? What's so important at a hock shop that you need to go right now?"

"Still looking for that ukulele, and I got a lead that it might be at Pete's on Waialae. You know anything about that place?" she asked. She thought she heard the sound of Christmas music in the background of the call.

"Only that there are more honest shops to do business with than his. You really need to go to his?"

"The pawn stub I have evidently came from his store, so, yeah."

"Take someone with you."

"Maybe my brother isn't busy," she said, more to herself.

"I hate to tell you this, but the Spencers aren't terribly menacing."

Maile chuckled at the idea of her little brother not being menacing. "He's barely menacing to the golf balls he swings at."

"Give Turner a call. He's off this evening."

"Brock?"

"Do you know another Turner?"

"Brian."

"Isn't he recovering from eye surgery?" Ota asked.

"Yeah. I need to call him anyway. Come to think of it, Pete's isn't far from Brock's place."

"Pete's in Kaimuki? That's halfway across town from where Brock is living."

Maile was confused for the tenth time that day. "He lives just off Waialae, within a couple of blocks of Pete's, barely around the corner."

"Oh, yeah, that's right. Maybe you should give him a call."

With that, Detective Ota was off the call, leaving Maile alone to figure out what to do with the pawn stub.

Chapter Twelve

Maile had a decision to make: take the bus to Kaimuki and demand answers from Pete the pawnbroker, or go home. She was tired of taking buses back and forth across central Honolulu, but she wanted to get to the bottom of the story behind the pawn stub in her hand. She still wasn't sure Reverend Ka'uhane's ukulele had been stolen, or had been accidently taken by someone. At that point, recovering the ukulele was almost secondary to the twists and turns she'd been following since it disappeared from the potluck. In only a few days, the case of the ukulele had become as complex as Oscar Swenberg's disappearance.

"Yeah, the Swenberg secret," Maile said to herself as she went to a bus stop to wait for a ride across town. "What am I supposed to do with that?"

There was a trendy coffee house where she got off the bus, and she went in for a jolt of energy. While she sat in the window watching people pass by on the sidewalk and cars stream back and forth, she made a decision. Directly across the street was Brock's apartment, just half a block up Koko Head Avenue. If she went over unannounced and uninvited, she might be interrupting a quiet evening at home. She'd also be able to visit with Brian to see how his eyes were coming along, and rehash a few memories with Amelia about the marathon the week before. If Brock was there, she'd only need to borrow him for a moment to go to Pete's pawnshop just down the block. In fact, she could see that the lights were on in the shop, the sidewalk illuminated in front of it. A pair of young women came out of the shop, looking disappointed that whatever had been their scheme going in hadn't turned out well for them.

"Oh, who am I kidding? I came here to see Brock, not go to that stupid store."

She finished her coffee and left the café. Hurrying across the street to beat the changing signal, she decided to walk past the pawn store. Trying her best to look nonchalant about it, she looked in the store window as she passed it by. Pete was there examining something a customer had brought in with a single monocle. Another customer was there looking through the glass top of a display cabinet, and a pair of young women were tapping their fingernails on yet another case pointing at something of desire.

Instead of doubling back to pass in front of the store again, she crossed the street and pretended to window-shop. Watching the pawnshop in secret from that side, Maile made the decision to cross back over and go to Brock's apartment to ask for help.

"Yeah, I don't look stupid, crossing the same street. Seriously, I could be at Mom's house, drinking cider or hot chocolate. Instead, I'm casing a pawnshop. I wonder if people still use that word?"

She walked a little heavily as she climbed the steps to Brock's second floor apartment, hoping to announce her presence before knocking. When the door was answered, it was Amelia peeking through the chained gap with her unseeing eyes.

"Hi Amelia. Sorry to show up like this. Is Brock here?"

"Maile!" The blind woman fussed over the chain until it was released and let Maile in. "Why aren't you at a Christmas party?"

"Maybe because I wasn't invited to any. Is Brock here? I just need to borrow him for a few minutes."

"It's his day off. He hasn't been here since this afternoon. Why? Is there a problem?"

"Not really a problem." Brian showed up then. They talked about his eyes, him bragging about his newly restored vision and pretending to now have X-ray vision. They were barely noticeable, but Maile could just see the tiny sutures that held the grafts in place. They all had a seat, since that was the biggest thing in his recovery, to be careful and rest his eyes as much as possible. "Maybe you've heard about the ukulele that went missing at the potluck a while back. I think I know where it is, and I just need Brock to go with me."

"As muscle or as a police officer?" Amelia asked.

"Maybe a little of both. I'm pretty sure the ukulele is at a pawnshop just around the corner from here." She explained about the run-around she'd been on all afternoon, and showed the ticket stub for the instrument. "If I don't find it there, I'm giving up. Reverend Ka'uhane will just have to live without it."

"Maybe you can buy him a new one for Christmas?" Brian offered.

"Good idea, at least until I found out how expensive they are. I'm still waiting for a few bills to be paid to the tour company before I start spending much money. Honestly, I'm not sure how long I can keep it open. I'm terrible at sales, and I have no business sense at all when it comes to running an office."

"Maybe I can help?" Brian said. "You said a while back that you need an office manager. "I've had office experience in the past before I was in the service. I've been running my own little businesses, even while blind."

"Are you applying for the job?" she asked. "Your eyes still need to recover."

"I can see well enough to use the computer here. Once the stitches are out and I'm fitted for glasses, I'll be ready to go."

There was a ray of hope. "Well, it's not much of a company. I have only four employees and two vans, plus the office that I rent. There would be the books to balance, payroll to deal with, and sales calls to make. Is that something you could deal with?"

"I led a platoon of soldiers in combat. I think I can deal with tour guides and bus drivers."

Maile chuckled about Susan and her past, and whatever it was between Lopaka and Ota that was still being kept secret from her. "You haven't met them yet."

"Can you afford another employee?" Amelia asked.

"I could afford to pay Brian guide wages, but not office manager wages, at least until business picks up a little."

"What about a minimum wage sales woman to make calls?"

"Do you have someone in mind?"

"Me?" Amelia asked.

Maile gave it some thought. She could use someone dedicated to making sales calls and follow-up thank yous. "I don't know how that could work. None of my computers are set up for voice command."

"That's not hard to do. I bet at least one of them have the capability, if the right program is found. We could come in on Monday morning and work on that."

"It sounds like you're trying to talk your way into jobs?" Maile asked.

"Is it working?" Amelia asked.

Maile had a little more than a week before she left town and she needed to find someone to run the business. As it was, no one had answered her ads for an office manager yet, or to buy the place.

"Okay, you're hired," she said with a sigh. At least one problem had been solved.

"Both of us?" Amelia asked.

"If you can figure out how to make one of the computers work for you at the office, the job is yours. Both of you need to be at the office by eight in the morning on Monday so you can meet the group before they go out on tours." She gave them business cards and the best bus route to take to get there. "Any idea when Brock will be home?"

"Are you expecting him here?" Brian asked.

"Eventually."

"You do know he no longer lives here, right?"

"Huh?"

"He moved out a few days ago and we assumed his lease."

"Where's he staying?" Maile asked.

"You don't know?" Amelia asked.

"I have no idea what's going on with him from one day to the next."

"It might be best if he tells you himself," Brian said. "We're not expecting him this evening, though."

"Mind if I hang out here while I call him?" she asked.

"Okay with us," Amelia said. "We were just watching TV."

"Okay." Maile got out her phone, wondering if her new friend was making a joke.

"Nobody ever gets that," Amelia said.

When Brian started to explain to Amelia about how her joke no longer made sense because he could now see, Maile stepped away to talk to Brock.

"Hey, where are you?"

"At home. What's up?"

"That's great, but you're not at the home I thought was your home."

"You're at Brian's place?"

"I dropped by because I needed to ask you a favor." She explained the zigzagging story of possibly tracking the ukulele to the pawnshop. "At least I think it's there. If not, I'm giving up on it."

"How does that involve me?" Brock asked.

"Everybody I talk to says it would be a good idea to take someone with me, in case there's trouble. People get in trouble in pawn stores?"

"All the time. Any place that's busy swapping stuff for cash draws all sorts of characters, and they bring some pretty questionable schemes with them. That's why the owners of those places keep a piece under the counter."

"A piece as in a gun?" she asked.

"Right. And Pete seems to draw some of the most questionable dudes Honolulu has to offer. I've been in his shop a couple of times to settle disputes, as have most patrol officers in town. Half the time it ends in someone going to the station in cuffs. You really want to go in there? Just for an ukulele?"

"I'm right around the corner from the place. I just want to put it to rest, you know?"

"Give me a few minutes to get there and I'll go in with you."

"Dressed like a cop?"

"No, but I might flash my badge, if it comes to that."

Once Maile was off the call, she began quizzing Brian about his vision again, even checking his eye drop schedule.

"You're being careful with your blood pressure and not taking any unnecessary risks with exertion?"

"He hasn't exerted himself with me since before the operation, if that's what you're asking," Amelia said.

"Well, no, that's not…I meant…maybe I should wait outside for Brock." Maile made a jailbreak of her own out the door and down the steps. "I need to stop dropping in on people."

Brock parked around the corner, close to his old place. It looked as though he purposefully parked aimed at the main street, even with his wheels angled out toward traffic.

"Okay, have you thought about how you're going to approach this guy?" he asked when they met.

"I just want to show him the pawn stub and ask to buy the thing."

"You have the stub?"

She handed it over to him. After looking at both sides, he gave it back.

"I was told that whoever has this stub can claim the item, pay off the loan, and walk out with it, no questions asked," she said.

"That's how it works, generally. These guys are slippery, though. He's in the business of making as much of a profit off merchandise, and people, as possible. How long has he had it?"

"Only a few days, since the potluck. Why?"

"There's a waiting period if someone other than the owner wants to buy the thing, but since you have the stub, you should be able to get it."

"Why is the stub so important?" she asked.

"Whoever has the stub can be considered the owner of the hocked item. That's what makes the situation so interesting, is that you got the stub from a music store owner for an instrument that was hocked at a pawnshop. There's no telling what might happen with this deal."

"That's not very reassuring, you know that?" she said.

The shop was busy when they went in, with Pete trying to manage several customers at once. He was just taking a bracelet from a young woman's hand and putting it away when Maile approached.

"I thought I'd see you again," he said, after a quick glance at Maile, and then at Brock, who was milling around at the opposite side of the store.

"Why'd you lie to me the other day when I came in here?"

"Lie?"

"You told me you don't have the ukulele for sale that I was looking for. I even showed you a picture of it."

"That wasn't a lie. It wasn't for sale. It's collateral for a loan I made to someone."

She waved the pawn stub in front of him. "I have this, and that entitles me to buy it, right?"

"Not buy, but pay off the loan, along with a few fees. That's assuming you have the right ticket for it."

When she handed over the stub, he got out a ledger book and searched a few pages. Tapping his finger on one specific listing, he slammed the book shut again. "Already gone out the door."

"What? How?"

"Someone bought it."

"For the ten thousand you quoted me?"

"Hundred bucks, cash."

"How could you do that? You told me I'd need to come up with ten thousand dollars if I wanted to buy it!"

Their argument had a way of clearing out the small shop, and bringing Brock closer.

"Take a guess why, little Miss Sunshine."

"What'd you just…do you have the ukulele or not?"

"I just told you it went out the door about an hour ago."

"Do you have a sales record for the buyer?" Brock asked. He was now standing next to Maile.

"Who're you? Why do you care about it so much?" Pete asked.

Brock flashed his badge. "Show us the sales slip or I close you down, and with all the customers that have been in here this evening, I doubt you want that. You know, right before Christmas. This is a busy season for you right?"

Pete made a show of looking through another ledger, before going to a box of slips that might've been receipts. "It's around here somewhere."

"Sound like another one of your lies to me," Maile said, her hands on her hips.

"Seems to have gone out the door in a hurry. Was it here in the shop for the full waiting period, and for the police department to verify it hasn't been stolen, just like all merchandise that comes in here?" Brock asked.

"Look, pal. You can come in here flashing your badge all you want. Just like you said, this is a busy time of year for me. So what if I fudge on dates a little? Did anyone get hurt? No. It's not like I sold her granny's heirloom wedding ring."

Brock leaned his weight on the counter between them. "Start cooperating or I close your doors and call a team to check your books against your merchandise, including what you have in the safe."

"Okay, look," Pete said, throwing his ledger onto his little desk. "I don't have everything here. Only the good stuff. I don't have the space for a bunch of crappy guitars."

"Not a guitar," Maile hissed. "Where is it?"

"All the big stuff is at my house. I can't sell the thing because it's still in the waiting period, okay? So, you see? You can't shut me down."

Brock snatched the ticket from Maile's hand. "We have the stub. We want to claim the item for ourselves. Whoever has the ticket can get it back. That's the law, waiting period or not."

"I just told you, it's not here. Come back tomorrow and I'll have it ready for you."

That seemed to satisfy Brock, but not Maile. "Forget it. You've been lying to me right from the beginning, and you're still lying now. I want that ukulele! Tonight!"

That cleared the last two customers from the store. Even Brock eased away from her side a little.

Pete seemed to give it some thought. "Okay, fine. Take the ticket to my house, along with a hundred bucks. Give the ticket and money to my wife and she'll hand over the uke. Okay?"

"Where's your house?" she asked.

"Not required to tell you that. Find it for yourself. Might be quicker and easier if you wait until I open in the morning."

It was Maile's turn to lean her weight on the counter top. "You're not telling me your address?"

Brock took her by the arm and pulled her from the store. "Forget that guy, Mai. Never mind about the ukulele. It's not worth all this."

She pulled her arm away. "It is to me."

"What do you want to do, drive all over town looking for a pawnbroker's house?"

"If you don't want to help, you can go home."

They went back to the coffee house she'd visited earlier and got more to drink. Finding a table, she got out her phone and pulled up data. Plugging in the name of the business in a search bar, she found the website for Pete's shop.

"Okay, Pete's last name is apparently Gallagher. All I have to do is find out where Peter Gallagher lives in Honolulu."

"Pretty common name, even for Honolulu."

"I might get lucky. Do pawnbrokers make a lot of money?"

"Why?"

"It lets me know in what part of the island he might live," she said.

"Good idea. Ones with larger shops than his could do well. I got the idea there's more business going on in there than hocking jewelry and cameras. How many Gallaghers are there?"

"Not all that many, and only one Peter," she said, scrolling up and down in a people finder site. "You know what? His address isn't too far from here."

"I thought you were giving up on your wild goose chase if he didn't have it?"

"He just told us where to go, and how much to pay."

"He told us where to go, alright. He's also called half a dozen of his buddies to meet us there."

"You're a cop. What can he do? Can't beat us up."

"Seriously? You're that naïve? Cops are magnets for that sort of thing. Every brother on the island with a chip on his shoulder would love the chance to beat up a cop."

Maile barely listened while looking at the little internet map on her phone. "He lives on Sierra Drive. If we follow Wilhelmina Rise, that crosses Sierra a couple of times. Do you know it?"

"Sierra and Wilhelmina cross several times. I used to go running up there on days off."

They went to Brock's truck and got in. Maile put away her phone and dropped her bag on the floor, keeping only the pawn stub in her hand. "Good. You know where to take us."

"I don't have every house number memorized. I only know where the dogs live."

"Just drive. We're in a pickup truck. How dumb does a dog have to be to chase after a pickup?"

"Not only are these family pets, some are guard dogs, and others are hunting dogs. If they'll chase after a feral boar with giant tusks, they'll chase after anything, including police officers driving pickup trucks," Brock said as he eased the pickup along slowly. They were both searching for address numbers as Sierra Avenue wound its way through the dark neighborhood. "What's the address again?"

"I think we're on another wild goose chase," Maile said. "We just passed street numbers for neighbors on either side of him."

"Some of these driveways lead back to other houses in back."

"Maybe there's another part of Sierra back there?"

"I doubt it. There's a wilderness park behind these houses, with a couple of trails and gullies. Fun to explore." He passed one area where they could see back into the trees.

"Fun to explore, if you're filming a Hawaiian-style Blair Witch Project movie," Maile said, getting a shiver.

"I'm going to double back. I think we just went past it."

Brock left his pickup parked in the street, angled downhill. Both of them went down a long driveway alongside a house. Most of the lights were off in the houses, with TVs flickering blue light off walls.

Conversations from neighbors on either side were easily heard. Once they got to the door of a large house in the back, they listened as a dog barked at them from inside.

"Is this the right address?" he asked before knocking.

"I think so."

"Check it on your phone."

"I left that in your truck in my bag. I'm sure it's right," she said, before rapping her knuckles on the door. The knocking seemed to incite even more barking from the dog.

"Yeah?" a woman asked inside, without opening the door.

"Is this Pete's house?"

"You the ones looking for the ukulele?"

"Yep."

"I don't have it."

"Pete just sent us here to get it," Maile said over the noise of the barking dog.

"Pete can get his own ukulele."

"Look, we know you're his wife, and we know you have the ukulele in there. We have a hundred bucks, which is what Pete wants for it."

"Good for Pete, but he ain't here," the woman said. The dog still wasn't settling, and the woman wasn't trying to shut it up.

"Pretty simple deal," Maile said. "I give you a hundred dollars cash and you give me the ukulele. Transaction done."

"What if the transaction ain't done that way?"

"We stand here and keep banging on the door until you open up!"

"I'll call the cops."

"The cops are already here." Brock waved his badge at the peephole in the door. "If you want to bring even more police here, fine with me. We can search the entire house for the instrument, and anything else we find will be held against you as evidence. How's that sound?"

"Not very good. I mean, this ain't my house, it's Pete's."

"You're in it, he's not. Just heel your dog and open the door. Give us the ukulele and we'll leave you alone."

"Show me the money," the woman said through the door.

Maile held up the five twenty dollar bills she'd gotten from an ATM before going up the hill. With that, the security chain could be heard sliding across its track and the door eased open a little. With one hand firmly holding the dog's collar to keep it back, and her other hand holding the door, a woman with stringy red hair asked to see the money again.

"Where's the ukulele?" Maile demanded, keeping a firm grip on her money.

"In the back room. Come in a get it."

Maile started to take a step, but Brock restrained her. "Not with that dog in there."

"I'll put it out back."

"Forget it," Brock said. "There's no fence, which means the back yard and the front are the same. Go get the instrument."

The woman struggled keeping the dog back while it continued to bark and bare its teeth at Maile and Brock. "What's it look like?"

"Old, made from koa wood."

"What's koa wood?"

"Quit acting dumb and get the dang ukulele!" Maile shouted.

With that, driveway and backyard floodlights came on at the neighboring houses.

"Connie, you okay?" a neighbor shouted out the door. "Want me to call the cops?"

"That's who these dopes are, the cops trying to roust me out of here."

"We're not trying to roust you out," Brock said. Maile noticed his hand went under his jacket to behind his back. "We just want the ukulele."

"Connie, maybe you should call Pete!" the neighbor said, just as the floodlights went off again.

Maile held up the money again. "Hundred bucks for the ukulele. You have a minute to go find it and then we call for backup."

Connie sneered at them as much as the dog bared its teeth, just before she closed the door.

"We're calling for backup?" Brock whispered to her. "A little liberal, considering you're not a cop."

"Sorry. Just trying to force the agenda a little."

"We have an agenda?"

Maile smiled at him. "Yeah, get the ukulele one way or another."

"We're buying it. That's the only way."

The door opened again. This time, Connie had the ukulele in one hand and the dog in the other. Maile knew at first glance it was the right instrument. She held out the money for the woman to take, and got the instrument in her other hand.

"I should get a receipt for that," Maile said.

Connie looked confused. "A receipt?"

"Yeah. My name, your name, the date, a hundred bucks, ukulele. A receipt."

Connie made a show of rolling her eyes as she swung the door closed. Before it was closed completely, the dog lunged. Brock wasn't quite fast enough to grab the doorknob to close it before the dog broke free from Connie's grasp and leapt through the gap.

"Go!" Brock shouted.

Seeing the dog's teeth dripping with saliva aimed in her direction was all the incentive Maile needed to start running. As she bolted in one direction, Brock ran in the other. The dog, once again barking its head off, ran after Maile as she sped off into the dark.

Brock began shouting and whistling for the dog to come to him, as was Connie. Maile didn't wait around to see where it was going. She raced down the narrow walkway at the side of the house, aiming for what looked like a patio in the back. She was beyond the lights now, running through the dark as she crossed the concrete pad. The yelling and calling for the dog continued behind her, as the dog closed the distance between its teeth and Maile's flesh, its chain leash jangling on the ground.

She saw a low lava rock wall only a few steps in front of her. With no time to consider an alternative, and with the hot breath of a mad dog on the backs of her calves, she had to decide if she would hurdle the wall in one leap, or use it as a springboard to whatever lie beyond. In the near pitch black, she had no idea of what that was.

Taking one last step before leaping like an Olympic hurdler, she caught her toe on the top of the wall, propelling herself head first into the unknown. For some reason, she closed her eyes as she braced for impact.

Chapter Thirteen

Stars floated in her eyes when Maile's belly flop in the dirt ended. She'd landed on a slope and slid a little, softening the landing. Hearing the dog continue to bark only feet behind her, she wrenched her senses back to the trouble at hand.

The ukulele had tumbled forward. Pushing up from the dirt, she grabbed the musical instrument and started running again. To where, she had no clue. All she knew was that a dog with four legs and giant drippy teeth wanted to make a snack of her hind end. Running down the slope, she hoped she could stay ahead of the noisiest dog she'd ever come across. After a few more steps, firm dirt and grass turned to stones and rubble, with only tuft grass holding the hillside in place. A miniature landslide started, and instead of trying to avoid it, she ran through it, jumping and hopping over rocks until she came to a sudden stop.

It was a good thing she did, because scanning the moonlit terrain, she found herself on a rocky ledge, with a dark drop below. Maile looked behind her to see how the dog was faring with the hillside. It hadn't followed her, but was still barking its head off back at the house. Through the trees, she saw a pair of headlights wind their way down the curving road, and she figured it was Brock in his pickup. Listening closer, the barking seemed to be following him.

"Good for him. He's locked safe and sound inside a truck." She looked around the terrain again and got a shiver. "And I'm out here in Blair Witch Country."

Maile dusted the dirt from the ukulele, trying to see it closely for damage. She wasn't sure if the nicks and scratches were new, or were those of Reverend Ka'uhane's doing. She slung it over her shoulder, snugging the strap tight to her chest, leaving both her arms free.

"He better appreciate this." She chuckled as she looked for a way off her ledge. "Or what will I do? Not let him marry my mom?"

From the feel of her feet in the loose dirt on one side of the ledge, she could tell landslides were common along there. She half-walked, half-slid until she came to another stop in the large parkland. She tried remembering what she'd seen on the map of the green space. All that she could see with her mind right then was a large patch of woods with a trail that wound around, completely surrounded by residential neighborhoods that were slowly creeping up the volcanic slope. Deciding it was easily to go downhill that up, she pushed through shrubs and trees, hoping she'd find the trail without too much trouble.

Not all trees in Hawaii were as friendly as the people, though. Some had long thorns that in the middle of the night resembled dog fangs, snagging at her clothes, and digging into her skin as she tried to avoid them. It was almost as if they were reaching out to her with their branches and twigs full of woody spikes, turning the woods into a natural prison, dedicated to keeping her there.

"Yeah, this is fun. I could've gone Christmas shopping, bought Reverend a necktie, a bottle of perfume for Mom, and then sat around her house drinking cider." She gingerly pushed a branch aside to get through, letting it whip back once she was past. "But oh no, I have to go bushwhacking in Thorn City."

When she finally found the trail, there was a small wooden footbridge spanning a narrow creek. Stopping to wash her hands in the cool trickle that was tumbling down the narrow gorge, she splashed some on her face. Cupping her hands for more water, she washed her legs and arms. Scratches stung, and she heard the buzzing sound of mosquitoes looking for a meal. Slapping her neck, she knew it was time to keep going downhill.

After ten minutes of carefully following the winding trail that led back and forth across the stream several times, she heard a voice. She stopped to listen more intently. It was almost as if someone was speaking her name. It wasn't Brock calling from a distance, and she'd left her phone in his truck, but there was the definite sound of an odd voice speaking her name.

"Great. Now I'm hearing things."

She was lost in trees again, the trail having given out a moment before. Maile peered into the darkness, hoping to see what might be ahead of her, if a way through the trees could be found. All she could see were stars mostly hidden by tree branches. Taking a tentative step forward, she heard the voice again from somewhere in front of her.

"Mairee…Mairee…"

She brought her foot back and stood still. "Okay, who's that?"

"Mairee…Mairee…"

"Who's saying my name?" she asked the darkness. Shaking her head, she started to take a step again. "Hearing things."

"Mairee…Mairee…"

The voice was now behind her.

She turned around and peered back toward the trail she'd lost. "Brock is that you? If it is, this isn't funny!"

There was a flutter in a tree. A twig snapped. "Mairee…Mairee…"

It wasn't a human voice, not even a…

"Don't even think about ghosts," she muttered. She rubbed her arms more because of the chicken skin that was coming up than from the mosquitoes that continued to haunt her flesh.

There was another flutter in the trees. Catching only a glimpse of it, this time a white bird flew from one tree to another.

"Mairee…Mairee…"

She walked closer to the tree where she could see only the silhouette of a bird as it flapped its wings again.

"Mairee…Mairee…"

She did her best to see into the tree where the bird was hidden.

"King?"

The bird fluttered its wings and landed on a branch above her head. "Mairee."

"King!" She held her arm up to him. When he hopped down and landed on her wrist as he had always done, she knew it was King. She rubbed his face with her fingertip. "Why are you here? Where have you been for so long? I've been worried sick about you."

"Mairee."

"And why are you saying my name? You haven't spoken in years. Not even my name. Have you been staying in these woods all this time?"

He playfully bobbed his head up and down.

"Why didn't you come home? Couldn't you find your way?"

With one last head bob, he fluttered to the ground where he hopped forward a few feet.

"Now where are you going?" She watched as he continued to hop forward through the leaves. "Hey, I'm done sightseeing. I have to go home."

She turned around to go back to where she had been looking for the trail. Edging a foot forward in the dark, she found the edge of the stone she was standing on.

"Mairee…"

Maile knelt so she could feel the rock. What she found was a long edge, with a deep drop below. Picking up a pebble, she tossed it over the edge and listened for the impact of it on the ground. It took a couple of seconds before it hit.

"Okay, that's got to be thirty feet, at least."

"Mairee…" King called from behind her.

She crept back to where he was waiting on a branch. "Are you trying to warn me not to go that way? Is that what all the talking is about?"

King bobbed his head and fluttered his wings for a moment.

"Easy for you to just fly somewhere, but I don't have wings."

Acting as if he understood, King fluttered to the ground where he began to hop back into the woods.

"Okay, fine," she said, following him. "But if you lead me over a cliff, no more birdseed for you."

It took barely five minutes of following King as he fluttered from tree to tree to find her way out of the woodland park to a trailhead. That's where she found Brock's red pickup truck parked in a small lot. He was busy putting on a fanny sack with bottles of water.

"Where're you going?" she asked him. He looked startled to see her.

"To look for you." He went to where she stood and looked her over. "What happened to you?"

"Hawaii happened. Can I get a ride home, please?"

"Yeah, sure." He opened his pickup and helped her in. "What do you mean, Hawaii happened?"

She dabbed at a couple of scratches on her arms. "Let's just say I'm better suited to modernday Hawaii than the good old days of our ancestors."

He started the engine. "You want to go to the hospital to get checked out?"

"I'm okay. Hold on, though. We have another passenger."

"Mai, I'm not taking hitchhikers places."

"King!" she shouted. With that, King flew from one tree to the next, before landing on a railing. From there, he hopped down to the ground below her door, and then up to her out-stretched arm. She rubbed his nose. "Good boy."

"That's King? I thought he flew off?" Brock asked, driving away from the park.

"He did. I guess he's been waiting here for me."

"Okay." Brock took them straight down Wilhelmina Avenue, where they'd gone up two hours before. "How'd he know you were going to find him there?"

"I don't know. Maybe the same reason he knew I was going to walk off a cliff."

"Huh?"

She explained about King calling her name as a warning to stay away from the direction she was headed, and to follow him. "He's a pretty smart guy. Smarter than me, anyway."

"What makes you think that?" he asked.

"He knows how to fly and I don't."

After being prompted to take her to her mother's house, Brock got on the freeway. "You lead an interesting life, Maile Spencer."

"I'm ready for it to be a little more boring. What happened with Fang back there at the house? I can't figure out why it didn't chase after me."

"Pete has an invisible pet fence around his house, the kind that dogs won't cross. But the fence doesn't cover the front, so when it couldn't chase after you, it came after me. By then, I was in the truck, and the dumb thing chased me halfway down the hill."

"Did you lose him?"

"I turned around to lead him back home. Once he got there, Connie called him into the house. I think he was too tired to do any more chasing by then."

"Good for him. Not so good for me," she said, dabbing at a small thorn gash on her arm.

"You found King, though."

She rubbed the bird's beak. "More like he found me."

When they got to her mother's cottage, only one small light was on in the front window.

"I hope they haven't gone to bed already," she said as they parked. "I don't want to interrupt anything."

Brock started up the walkway. "You won't interrupt."

"I need to put King in his aviary and get him some seed. He must be starved." Maile went through the process of filling his food and water bowls while King watched from his highest perch. Once she was done, he fluttered his wings and dropped to the floor for a meal. After making sure he was enclosed securely, she went to the back door of the cottage. "I don't have my keys. They're in your truck in my bag."

When she returned to where he was waiting on the back porch, she watched as he unlocked and opened the door with a key of his own.

"How'd you get a key to my mom's house?"

"Your mother gave it to me."

"Why you? I know you're going to be helping out at the Manoa House, but you don't need to be in here for that."

Brock continued to turn on lights as he led her into the living room. Plugging in an extension cord, a Christmas tree began to twinkle with a few lights, the same one she had partially decorated earlier. "She gave it to me because I live here now."

Maile went to the tree and felt a few twigs. It was real. Not only that, most of the ornaments weren't Spencer family ornaments, but ones she'd never seen before.

"You live here with my mom?"

"No, I live here alone. Your mother has moved in with Reverend Ka'uhane."

"What? My mother is not living..." She stopped. "When did she move in with the Reverend?"

"A few days ago."

Maile dropped her bag on a chair that she recognized from Brock's old apartment, along with the ukulele. "Nobody ever said anything to me about it!"

"Remember when I said I was helping someone move?"

"That was my mom?"

He nodded. "Kenny helped."

"Good for him. How many other surprises do you guys have in store for me? And just exactly when was I going to be told about this?"

"Tomorrow, which is now today. Christmas Eve. They want to have Christmas Eve and Day at his place."

Having heard enough, Maile waved her hands for him to stop. "I need to take a shower. Maybe after that, something will make sense again. Okay if I use your bathroom?"

"Sure. There are towels in the linen cabinet next to..."

"I know where the linen cabinet is. I grew up in this house, remember?" She turned for what had been her bedroom in the past. "Are my things still here or have they gone to the donation center?"

"Your room is still the same, but without all of your mother's sewing stuff."

Maile found clean clothes for after her shower and went to the bathroom. Gone was her mother's stuff, along with her and Kenny's few things they kept there.

There were only the usual masculine things of shaving, after shave lotion, a fancy toothbrush, and a brand of minty toothpaste. Snooping a little more, she found aspirin and simple over the counter painkillers, antacid, and eye drops in the medicine cabinet. She found extra rolls of TP, an electric heating pad, and a first aid kit. Learning that much about Brock, she gave up on the scavenger hunt and took her shower.

At the end, she broke into the first aid kit for ointment and Band-Aids for her cuts and scratches left over from her escape through the woods. There was no skin lotion to wipe on, or a dryer for her hair. After getting dressed, she joined Brock in the kitchen where he'd made sandwiches and had poured glasses of milk. Even though none of her mother's things were there, none of the things she'd grown up with, the moment had a homey feel.

"You do realize that your neighbors are already gossiping?" she said.

"About what? I'm not very interesting."

"About having a woman here so late."

"But this is your house!"

"Not anymore. I'm a visitor, and it's close to midnight. "There's lots to gossip about with that."

"It's not like you're spending the night," he said. He took their empty plates and glasses to the sink. "Are you?"

"Would that be a problem? Because, no pun intended, I'm dog-tired. It's been a long day and ended with a mad dash through a thorn patch." She smiled as prettily as she could. "On the other hand, it could end with you giving my feet one of your award-winning foot rubs?"

"You know what that led to last time?" he asked.

"Yeah, me getting a good night of sleep."

"And to me listening to you snore all night." They met in the middle of the kitchen and embraced. "Staying the night won't cause issues with your mom?"

"Not her place. We've already figured that out. Anyway, it wouldn't be the first time a boy stayed the night."

"Sounds like there's some gossip in there?" he said after their lips parted.

"Nothing my mother ever found out about."

"Are you sure?"

"If she had, I'd still be grounded."

Chapter Fourteen

Brock's breakfasts weren't much different from Maile's, with coffee, cold cereal, and juice on the menu. Most of the meal small talk was about her mother's secret move to Reverend Ka'uhane's place, and why Maile had been excluded.

"I think most of the reason why she didn't tell you was because she didn't want to get a lecture about them living together before they were married," he said.

"She thinks I'm that much of a prude?"

"Sometimes people might get the idea you're a little old-fashioned."

"Why do they think that?"

"Maybe because of the way you dress. Sometimes."

"Look, I've been working as a tour guide the last year or so. I had to dress modestly. What's that got to do with anything?" she asked.

"I think when you show up at a potluck dressed like a missionary, people get the impression you're a little, I don't know, maybe..."

Saving Brock from going any further was the chime of a call on Maile's phone. She flashed him a look that they weren't done discussing it when she answered.

"Detective Ota, it's a little early, isn't it?"

"I need your help with something. Do you have an hour or two this morning?"

"There's a Christmas Eve service at the church I'm supposed to go to later, and I'd still like to do a little last minute shopping. After that, I'm going to put my feet up and fill my belly with hot apple cider. If some rum happens to spill into the cup, I wouldn't complain." Maile wondered what a police detective would need her help for, if it was a medical question about her old workplace at Honolulu Med, or some sort of Hawaiianna historical trivia. "What exactly do you need help with? I have a few minutes right now if you have a question about something in particular?"

"I'd need to take you somewhere for an eyes-on. After that, I'll take you wherever you need to go, I promise."

Maile checked the time. Brock was already washing the breakfast dishes, and they hadn't made any plans for the day. As it was, she didn't know if he was going to work later or not. After feeling a little insulted over being called a prude, she decided her time was better spent with Detective Ota. "Okay, you have two hours, starting now."

"Are you at home? Because I'm parked at the curb right outside your front door."

"I've already gone out."

"So early? You've turned into an early riser."

"Whether I want to be or not. Meet me at..." She wasn't sure of what to call the cottage now, if it was still known as her mother's place, or to call it Brock's new house. "...at the Manoa House. You know the place, right?"

"Right next to the cottage where your mother used to live, right?"

That answered that.

"Yeah. I'll wait for you in front."

Five minutes later, she kissed Brock goodbye for the day. Five minutes after that, she climbed into Ota's sedan and buckled in, taking Reverend Ka'uhane's ukulele with her. "Okay, where are you taking me, and what's this big question you have?"

"Just for a drive. I have you for another hour and fifty-eight minutes and plan to use them all."

"If this is what you do on your days off, maybe you should do it with Susan?" she asked.

"Not a day off, but I do need to talk to you about her."

"Why? Does she want to quit her job already? Because she's doing great." It hit Maile then what the problem was with Susan. "She isn't…"

"No. She likes her job. And for some reason, she likes being my daughter again."

"What's the problem, then?"

"How do I reward her for that?"

Maile chuckled. "You don't have to reward her at all. She's not a little kid any more. Believe it or not, your little girl has grown up, and expects to be treated like an adult. By me, by you, by everybody. What you should be asking is how not to screw that up."

"And how do I do that?" he asked.

"Not real sure. I mostly grew up without a father. Honestly, I'm a little in the dark about what fathers do."

"Well, I am one, and I'm not sure either. I feel like I should be doing something, though."

"Treat her like the young woman she is. A nice way to start would be to give her something personal for Christmas, something from a dad."

They were on the freeway now, headed away from central Honolulu. He talked about the gift he was planning to give his daughter, and Maile approved.

"Maybe in her free time she could do some volunteer work?" Maile suggested as they went past Pearl Harbor. "She'd meet a nicer class of people than what she's been hanging around with these last few years."

"You think she's ready for a boyfriend?"

"I think..." Maile watched as they exited the freeway, still wondering where they were going. She also wondered how to answer him. "Talking about your daughter is new territory for us. I'm not sure of how honest you want me to be?"

"Whatever gets me fewer surprises later."

"I think she should make a visit to a gynecologist's office to make sure everything is okay and have a few blood tests done before easing back into the dating scene."

"You're suggesting that as a professional nurse?"

"Yes, and as a woman, and as a sister to a little brother that has already been out on a date with her."

"Susan and Kenny have gone out?" he asked.

"Just to the movies. Honestly, I doubt you have to worry about Kenny. He's still a little afraid of girls. I'm not sure he knows what to do with them."

"I'm more concerned about what she'll do with him," Ota said, as he parked in an airport lot.

"Which is why she needs the blood tests. Why are we at the airport?"

"You're not being kidnapped. I just need you to see something."

"As in what? Is the duty free shop having a sale?" she asked.

"You'll see."

He led her directly to TSA where he flashed his badge and convinced the agent to let them through. From there, they continued on to the departures terminal for flights to the mainland. The terminal was busy with travelers going in every direction, some batched up in groups, others snoozing in seats. Maile checked her watch and half of their two hours were already used up.

"Detective, I need to be somewhere pretty soon."

"This is worth it if you're late."

He took her arm in his hand to lead her in one specific direction. The grip was a little too tight for her to pull free from. Then she noticed two men in police uniforms standing with someone between them. When she recognized who it was, she tried tugging her arm free.

"You bought me here to see him?"

"I think you need some closure, Maile."

"Give me your gun and I'll show you closure with that guy."

"Best not to say something like that to a police officer. That can land you in jail."

"The only person that needs to be in jail is that guy."

Maile was able to put the brakes on when a flight was called for that gate. All she really wanted to see was the man get on the plane and watch as it taxied to a runway. Maybe Ota was right, that she needed closure. Giving her arm one last tug, she broke free from his grip and hustled to where the cops were leading the man to the gate.

She grabbed him by the collar and pulled him around. "I want a word with you."

When the two police officers tried to pry her grip loose from his shirt, Detective Ota flashed his badge and waved them off. While other passengers walked past the scene to stand in the boarding line, watching them as much as the tickets in their hands, Maile set her jaw, ready for whatever fight might come along.

"Look, Mai…"

She stuck a finger in his face. "Don't call me that. Don't even say my name, you pathetic little jerk. Why aren't you in a jail cell with some big Samoan moke?"

"I can explain everything. I've already told the DA my side of the story and…"

"Robbie, save me the tears. I don't believe you and neither does anybody else on this island." She yanked the boarding pass from his hand. "Is this for a one-way ticket?"

"That's the deal I had to make, that I'd never return to Hawaii. If I do, I'll get picked up and put in jail."

She tossed the boarding pass back at him and stuck her finger in his face again. "Look, you little piece of excrement. If you ever show up here again, the problems you have with the police won't be nearly as bad as you'll have with me. Understand?"

Her ex-husband sneered, even laughed. "Or what will you do?"

She grabbed his ear and twisted it to bring him close so she could whisper to him. She pushed him back again as the airline agent was making the last call for Robbie's flight. "Remember that, and who said it to you."

With that, Maile turned on her heel and stormed away, Detective Ota trailing along behind. When she got to the curb outside, she had to wait for him.

"Where'd we park?"

"Wait here. I'll bring the car around."

A few minutes later, they were on the Nimitz Highway, headed back to town. Neither of them had said a word until now.

"Sorry," she mumbled.

"Don't worry about it. I was impressed, though."

"With?"

"You took the high road and didn't slap the daylights out of him," he said.

"I wanted to."

"What did you say to him at the end?"

"In his ear?" Maile told Ota the message.

He laughed. "I didn't know you knew words like that."

"I know a lot of words like that." She blotted an eye with a knuckle that was in danger of revealing her descending mood. "I just reserve them for special needs."

"You wouldn't be the first woman who's had a good cry in this car. A lot of men have also. It might wrap up the whole closure thing."

"Don't need to cry." She pressed a knuckle at the side of her eye again. "Not crying over that guy."

It was at a stop light when the dam burst. She put her hands over her face and let the tears run.

"I'm sorry. I guess it was a bad idea to take you there. I was trying to be helpful," he said, getting the car going again.

"I worked my butt to the bone to support that guy, and his stupid bar. Most of my paychecks went into that place, and into the bras of the women he hung out with behind my back. I always knew what was going on, but did my best to pretend I didn't. Every day, I'd cut my heart out for him, and never once did he ever thank me for it."

"He's gone. You'll never see him again."

Maile continued as if she hadn't heard him. "I cried myself to sleep almost every day over him. When I finally got smart and walked away, I promised I never would again." She shook her head, still trying to wipe tears away with the back of her hand. "Never crying over a man again."

By then, Ota was pulling to the curb in front of Maile's building. "You're going to be okay?"

She forced a smile. "I'm fine, really. I think I needed that more than I ever realized. Thanks for taking me there."

Instead of letting it idle, he turned off the engine. "What's the deal with Turner?"

"Brock? Nothing. Why?"

"Is there's nothing, why weren't you at home, and why did I pick you up at his house this morning?"

"Oh, that. You know he lives there now and that my mom has moved?"

"Half the department knows. There were a dozen officers that helped her move. I noticed you weren't there that day, though."

"Because nobody ever told me about it. It's supposed to be some big surprise," she said.

"Which begs the question, again, of what's the deal with Turner?"

"I guess I spent the night at his place last night."

"Is this a new development?" he asked.

"You sound like a gossipy old lady, Detective, but no, not so new. The problem is that I have a hard time staying awake, so officially, nothing has happened between us yet. Nothing worth gossiping about."

"What do you mean, nothing happened?"

"Not much different from that old movie, where the guy and gal sleep on opposite sides of a blanket they use as a curtain in a motel room. I dozed off on the bed and Brock slept on the couch." Maile chuckled. "You know what? He calls me old-fashioned, but he's as much of a gentleman as I am a prude, which might be a little too much. How do you like that for disclosure?"

"You're nothing if you're not honest, Maile."

"Thank you," she said with a simple head nod. "I'll take that as the biggest compliment someone can give me."

"You do understand that withholding your charms from a man is harmful to his psyche, right? He's not going to hang around too long waiting for you to somehow stay awake long enough to, I don't know…"

"Seal the deal? I know. We had a chat about this morning at breakfast. But he needs to realize I'm going out of town pretty soon. There's not much we can get started before then."

"It's definite you're leaving?" he asked.

"Yep. Everything is all arranged. I leave on the Second of January." She undid her seatbelt. "Gonna miss me?"

"Somehow, Honolulu won't be the same without you. Where are you going?"

She told him her plans and swore him to secrecy. "Somehow, I need to break it to my mother in a way she doesn't have a fit that I'll be so far away."

"My lips are sealed."

"Hey, let me ask you a question. How prudish am I?"

"Who called you that?"

"Specifically that, no one. But it's been implied by several people that I'm frumpy, or whatever."

"You have a way of being immune to flirtation, in giving or receiving it."

"You're saying be more like Susan?" she asked.

"Maybe halfway between you and her would be about right."

Maile nodded, knowing what to do. "Thanks."

Chapter Fifteen

Maile dressed for the Christmas Eve service at church. When she saw her image in the mirror, Ota's message about jazzing up her image came back to her, and she changed clothes into something somewhat less frumpy. Putting on a hat and stuffing her feet in a new pair of pumps, she left her little apartment.

After locking her door, she noticed the door across the hall from her slightly ajar. It was the Mendoza's old place, recently vacated. When she pushed the door open to look inside, everything was gone, right down to the bare floor. It was a poignant moment, no longer hearing her friend's voice scold the kids over a broken dish or toy, or an argument flare up between husband and wife, something that was always resolved by the end of the day. Backing out again, she closed the door and left.

"I promised Rosamie I'd come visit and bring a gift," she said, hurrying to the bus stop. "Why am I so busy on Christmas Eve? I should be sitting around getting tipsy on spiked cider at Mom's place."

She climbed aboard the next bus that stopped and found a seat near the exit door.

"Yeah, Mom's house. Now it's Brock's. Seems like someone could've mentioned that little change to me. I don't even know where my mother lives now. Reverend moved out of his apartment at the church so the new minister could move in. I never did hear where he moved."

She watched as a group of college girls coming from shopping at the mall climbed aboard and found seats toward the back. Checking out their fashions, she wondered how she compared on Brock's Frump-o-Meter. As she continued to evaluate their style of clothes and hair, Maile decided to give her mother a gentle earful about not telling her she was moving in with Reverend Ka'uhane.

When she got to the church, it was with only a few minutes before the special service was scheduled to start. The doorway was decorated with colorful lei and flowers, with one especially long garland woven from what had to be dozens of ti leaves. The few people outside were dressed well, and greeted her with true happiness in their voices.

"Wonderful day, Maile!" they'd each say as she went inside.

"Yep, Christmas Eve."

Before she could even walk toward the left side of the chapel to where she and her mother and brother usually sat, she stopped in her tracks. More flowers decorated the center aisle between the pews, and stands of flowers were on either side of the altar at the front. Off to one side sat a man strumming easy music on a guitar.

"Is someone getting married?" she mumbled, trying to remember if she'd received an invitation.

Shrugging it off, she went to where she normally sat and eased down. Neither Kenny nor her mother were there yet. Otherwise, the place was packed for the service. Just as she was flipping through pages in the hymnal, someone tapped her on the shoulder. "Mai, come. We need your help."

"Auntie Kelani." Maile put the hymnal away, followed her aunt, and then whispered, "Hey, who's getting married?"

"You'll see."

They got to a small classroom ordinarily meant for preschoolers on Sunday mornings. Going in, several women were there fussing over another. After a couple more steps, she noticed the woman of honor was her mother.

"Mom, what's going on?"

"What's it look like, Maile girl? Getting married today."

"Who is?"

"Me!"

Maile began to rearrange the multiple layers of lei over her mother's shoulders. "To Reverend Ka'uhane?"

"I hope so! Otherwise, both of us are in trouble!"

The other women departed, leaving Maile alone with her aunt and mother.

"I don't understand. Why are you getting married today? Reverend is supposed to be holding a special Christmas Eve service today."

"That's the special service, Mai," her aunt said.

"What do you mean?"

"Maile girl, we've been planning this for quite a while, but could never decide when. Then when Christmas approached, and with you going out of town soon, we decided today would be perfect. It's Ka'uhane's way of handing over the duties to the new minister, by holding our wedding."

"Why didn't you tell me? Maybe I wanted to be included!"

"Girl, with all the things you've been doing lately, you would've been too busy. And all that police work you've been doing has been stressing you out. That's not any fun for any of us."

"Stressing me out?"

"See how sensitive you are right now?"

"I'm not being…" Maile shook the nerves from her hands. "Okay, what can I do?"

"We're just waiting for the minister to tell us Ka'uhane is ready and we'll start," Aunt Kelani said.

"Who's his best man?"

"Keneka."

"Kenny's best man? He's barely a man. How can someone with acne be best man for anyone, let alone Reverend Ka'uhane?"

"Might be time for you to think of something else to call him. He'll be your dad pretty soon."

"Yeah, just what I need. Another nutty relative." Maile tried rubbing away the headache that was starting. "Who is your maid of honor?"

"I am," Aunt Kelani said. "You don't mind, do you?"

"Be my guest. I just wish someone might've told me a little earlier so I could've dressed for a wedding."

"You look fine. Maybe you'll turn a few heads with your outfit," Kelani said, before she sent Maile back out to take a seat.

It turned out to be a simple ceremony, with the new minister stumbling through the rites, even getting a couple of snickers from the congregation. It was another surprise after the ceremony that the reception would be held the next day, after Christmas service. Dozens of pictures were taken before the newly wedded couple left in a car that had been decorated with ribbons fluttering in the wind as they drove off.

Just as Maile was turning to find her brother to give him the scolding he deserved over not telling her about the wedding, Brock showed up at her side.

"Did that inspire you to get married again?" he asked with a smile on his face.

"Not after this morning, no." Maile saw Detective Ota dressed differently from that morning. He seemed out of place in his suit and necktie, since he wasn't a member of the congregation. "Hold on a minute."

When Maile closed in on him, Ota tried moving away, excusing himself through the crowd. She caught up with him anyway.

"Nice service," he said.

"Don't give me that. What are you doing here and why didn't you tell me about this?"

"Your mother's wedding? I thought you knew? Why wouldn't you?"

"Somehow, it was Honolulu's biggest secret." She watched as her Aunt Kelani came to them and took Detective Ota's arm as if they were there together. "Apparently, not the only secret in town."

They chatted for a few minutes, until Maile decided she'd had enough family time. When she found Brock, he was near the near the entrance talking to a pair of young women, who were busy asking him about his police career. It was her turn to take him by the arm, and she led him outside.

"What happened this morning?" he asked as he let her into his pickup.

"Detective Ota happened. He took me to the airport to wave goodbye to Robbie forever."

"And that was bad?"

"Everything was fine, until I had a nervous breakdown, and proceeded to treat everyone at the airport to a recap of our marriage. Then when Ota was driving me home, I promptly had another nervous breakdown in the front seat of his car. Right now, I'm this close to having my third breakdown of the day."

"Over?"

"Surprise wedding of the year, and the equally big surprise of learning Detective Ota is dating my auntie."

"You didn't know about that?" Brock asked.

"No. How long has that been going on behind my back?"

"Since she visited at Thanksgiving. That's why she put her Maui condo up for sale and is moving back here to Honolulu."

"So they can be together?" Maile found an aspirin in her bag and washed it down with a bottle of water. "I need to get out more often. I'm missing too much of the Spencer family soap opera."

Brock parked at the curb in front of Maile's building. "What are you doing for the rest of the day?"

"I still need to do some shopping and go to a friend's house for a while. Then maybe an errand downtown. Why?"

"Errands on Christmas Eve?"

"Back to work bright and early on Monday morning. I need to do them sometime."

"You're leaving town soon. I thought maybe we could spend some time together before you go?"

"Doing?" she asked.

"I don't know. Early dinner somewhere nice?" he asked.

"We'd need reservations for anywhere on a holiday. Anyway, isn't it a little late to get something started between us?"

"Better late than never, right?"

"Yeah, maybe. How about I give you a call later this evening?" she offered.

"I work tonight starting at seven. That's why I suggested an early dinner."

"Tell you what? You find me a hardware store in Kaimuki and I'll buy you lunch at the classiest place we can find."

"Classy in Kaimuki? Everything there is local. Or McDonald's."

"What's wrong with McDonald's? But first, we need to make a stop at a friend's house." When they left the hardware store, they had two bags each of tree ornaments, lights, and decorations. Back in his truck, Maile checked the Mendoza's address. "Okay, it looks like they live near McDonald's. That's convenient."

Brock eased the pickup down a narrow alley until they found the house address. "Not very big."

"Heck of a lot bigger than that little apartment they used to live in. Cute little neighborhood, too. Big trees for shade, and their church is nearby. Nice place to raise the kids."

"It sounds like you're nesting."

"Not yet, but someday."

They spent two hours at the house, getting tours from the parents of the inside, and tours of the outside from the kids. Maybe the most fun was when the tree was redecorated with the new ornaments Maile and Brock had brought, and watching the kids put up Santa and Frosty decorations around the front door. With time running short and Brock eventually needing to go to work, Maile gave Rosamie a hug goodbye.

"Not the same without you guys in the building," Maile told her friend.

"I wonder how long it'll be before Ol' Lady Taniguchi finds an occupant for our place?"

"With my luck, it'll be one of Happenstance's workmates that'll move in across the hall from me."

"Just more gossip!" Rosamie said. "Hey, you never did tell me where you're going?"

Maile whispered the job that was waiting for her in Rosamie's ear. "But don't mention it to anyone else for a few days, including Brock. I want to surprise him with it."

"Lips are sealed! And you'll be great with that. Come see us when you come back to Honolulu."

When Maile and Brock got to McDonald's across the street, they got a surprise. Brian and Amelia were there at a window table toward the front. They took their tray of food, Brock's burger and Maile's two packages of fries, and joined them.

"We walked here today, and neither of us needed a cane!" Amelia said.

"It's strange being able to lead her around now," Brian said.

"Your vision is that good already?" Brock asked.

"There're some funny halos around things, but better than before. I'll need glasses, but I can live with this."

"You guys are still set for starting work at the office on Monday morning?" Maile asked after Brian's good news had been hashed over several times.

"I'm ready for my life to get back on track," Brian said. "It'll be odd having to deal with computers using vision instead of voice prompts, though."

Maile chuckled. "If you like odd, wait till you see my bookkeeping. That'll make your day."

When Brock left the table to get rid of trays, Brian leaned forward to whisper to Maile. "Okay, what's the big secret about your new job?"

"Why don't you just get a new job here in town, Maile?" Amelia asked. "It's almost as if you're leaving town in shame."

"No shame. Maybe a little embarrassed, but I'm not ashamed of anything I've done. I just want a fresh start and see a few new things. Brian was a big inspiration for it. Both of you, in fact."

"Why me?" he asked.

"I guess all your problems with the VA system, having to wait so long. That just didn't seem right. I felt like there was more I could do." She shrugged. "Maybe after only a few years of working as a nurse, it was already getting a little boring. I'm looking forward to doing something different for a while."

"Which is what?" Brian asked.

Maile told them about her plans, and where she was going. "I leave right after the new year. Totally scared out of my wits, though."

"You're perfect for that, Maile."

"Perfect for what?" Brock asked when he got back to the table.

"Just talking about the tour company," Amelia said.

"Ready to go?" Maile asked Brock. "You said you need to get some rest before your shift, and I still have one more place to go. Can I get a lift to downtown?"

On their way out the door, Maile took one last glance at Brian and Amelia at their table, still acting like lovebirds.

"Think they'll stay together?" Brock asked once they were out in traffic.

"Brian and Amelia? I hear wedding bells ringing, brah. From what I saw, you're gonna be Uncle Brock pretty soon.

"Where am I dropping you?"

Fort Street mall. I want to do some window-shopping and have one more place to go."

"I can take you straight there if you like?" he offered.

"I'm still trying to stretch some of the kinks from my legs from the marathon, and that little jaunt through the woods the other night didn't help. Anyway, I just have a couple of places to go that you don't need to know about."

"Your mother is right. You keep too many secrets."

"Unlike you and half of Honolulu keeping my mother's wedding a secret from me?"

"She swore us to it," he said.

"Not like it would've been the first time a Spencer family secret was shared."

"Mai, if a kahuna tells you to keep something secret you obey."

"You know she's kahuna?"

"I don't know how, but I have since I was a kid. Most of the people at the Manoa House do."

Maile shifted nervously against the seatbelt. "What about Reverend Ka'uhane? Does he know?"

"I'm sure he does. Look, it doesn't matter if people know, Maile. The rest of us are okay with it. We know she's not going to perform witchcraft."

"It's not witchcraft and she's not a witch. That's why she keeps it quiet, so people don't start saying those kinds of things about her."

"Okay, let's get off that. Are you giving the Reverend his ukulele as a gift?"

"Yep. I don't know how to wrap it, though."

"Just a bow should be good enough."

"What about you? Are you dropping in their place after your shift in the morning?" she asked.

He pulled his truck to the curb where she pointed. "More of a family time thing, and I'm not family."

She patted his thigh. "Brah, you're as much of a family member as anybody could ask."

Not knowing how to say goodbye, she leaned over to kiss him. That turned into something much more passionate than the quick peck she had planned, and they didn't stop until the car behind them tooted its horn.

Maile walked down the outdoor commercial and shopping mall, looking at the fanciful decorations. "Okay, now for some last minute Christmas shopping and a little surprise for everyone."

Chapter Sixteen

When Maile left the shop, a place she'd known for ages but had never been in, her purchase was tucked at the bottom of her bag beneath her umbrella, bottle of water, and bag of snack chips. It had been a splurge, and she wasn't sure if Brock would appreciate it in the manner she meant it, but there it was, in its little box decorated with a red ribbon. The big question now was how to give him such a special gift.

It wasn't much of a walk to get to Chinatown. She walked past the bar that she now owned, which was being managed by the old bartender that had been there for years. She went in and handed over an envelope, his Christmas bonus.

"Not much going on in here," she said, looking at empty tables.

"If I were you, I'd unload it," Ace said. He was a little on the straggly side, with long white hair, beard, and a leather biker vest. She never had known why he was called that, and assumed it had something to do with his Vietnam War service. "This British pub thing ain't catching on."

"That was kind of a lame idea. What about you?"

"I can retire any time. I've just be hanging on here watching the soap opera between you and Rob. Now I don't even have that."

Maile chuckled. "Sorry to disappoint you. I was thinking of selling."

Ace began polishing glasses with a bar towel. "Fine by me. The next owner can hire new blood if they don't like the looks of me. When would you sell?"

"As soon as I can find a buyer. Just don't leave me high and dry."

River Street was only a block away, her last destination for the day. As she walked, she thought of her mother and her new stepfather now on their Christmas Eve honeymoon, and what that mean for them. Feeling embarrassed over just thinking about it, she put their private business out of her mind.

One side of River Street overlooked a storm drainage canal, but it meandered a little and always had water in it, making it more scenic than utilitarian. On the opposite side were small shops, something of a little Hanoi that was springing up. She knew the manager of at least two of the places, one of which she was headed to. When she got to a small Vietnamese noodle shop first, she went in, hoping to find a young woman that had been more of a business partner in the past than a friend.

Inside the small diner, every table was packed, and others were waiting impatiently to sit. Maile thought back to the first time she'd been in the place almost a year before, when they were more empty seats than patrons to put in them. Now the place was over-flowing with business.

"Is Binh here?" she asked a harried waitress.

"No Binh today," the new waitress told her. She wore a tight green T-shirt and shorts that left little to the imagination.

"Is she at the flower shop?"

The woman pointed. "Binh at salon. Busy there today."

Maile decided against ordering a pair of spring rolls to go, and went to the salon two doors down, another place Binh managed. Maile never had figured out if the girl barely out of her teens owned the places or managed them for someone else, businesses turning them into goldmines, from the looks of the people waiting to be served.

The salon was as busy as the pho diner, with women seated in both chairs having their hair done, and both nail stations busy. Even the small massage room door was closed, with a privacy sign hanging from the doorknob. She went past three other women waiting in chairs lined up in the front window to where Binh was working on a set of nails.

"Hey, do you have time for me today?" Maile asked after being greeted by all the stylists in the place.

"Seriously? You need to make an appointment. Everybody's trying to look their best for Christmas parties tonight."

"Yeah, you look busy. I have a business proposition to talk to you about, though."

"See those ladies waiting? They're business, money in the till. That's the kind of proposition I'm interested in."

Maile studied Binh's impossibly big eyes and glossy hair, and then looked at the customers waiting. She knew that if anyone could turn around her bar and make it profitable, Binh could. "I just need a few minutes."

"I'm almost done with these nails, and since I don't do hair, we can talk then."

Maile waited outside in the sunshine, letting a few winter rays warm her face. When Binh came out to join her, she hid in the shade of the awning. "What's your big proposition?"

"I own a bar, just a couple of blocks over. The place hasn't seen a profit in months. When I see all the customers waiting in line here at the salon, at the pho shop, and at the flower store, I know you're the one responsible for that."

"What bar?"

"That place decorated like a British pub."

"That dive?" Binh shook her head. "Maile, you're a nice lady and have really helped out my family a lot. Sorry, but I'm not interested in managing that dump for you."

"I don't want you to manage it, I want you to buy it."

"We don't have the money to buy something like that. Sure, we're in the black with each business, but we're not stuffing our bras with hundred dollar bills to stay warm at night."

"I don't know what that means, but whatever. I think you might have enough to buy it."

"What makes you think that?"

"I know you still have that gold bar I gave you a few months ago."

"Yeah, I have it hidden. It's our fallback, emergency money if we need it. So?"

One of the stylists came out and barked at Binh in Vietnamese. She barked back.

"Look, I'm not interested in owning or running a bar," Maile said. "And no one has responded to my ads to buy it. Are you interested or am I wasting my time?"

"That gold bar is worth about twenty-five grand, if I got full price for the weight, and I wouldn't. Your bar, or any business down here is worth a lot more than that, even a dive bar with no customers. Why are you giving it away so cheap?"

"I'm going out of town for a while, and don't want to deal with forms that need to be signed long distance. I just want to get rid of it, and giving it away cheap is my best chance for that."

"You're not much of a businesswoman, Maile."

"Nope. That's why I want to get rid of it. Even if I had the time, I wouldn't know how to turn it around into a profitable business."

"I'm supposed to trade my gold bar for your dive bar?"

"Yep."

"No other payments, no loans, nothing?"

"No strings attached," Maile said.

The stylist came out to shout at Binh again.

Binh seemed to do some calculations in her head while Maile and the stylist waited for an answer.

"Look, go in and check out the place. Think about it for a few days. I'll come back next weekend and we'll talk about it some more," Maile said.

Binh sent the stylist away. "I don't need to think about. You want to trade your bar for mine? I have that right?"

"Right. I don't know what kind of taxes need to be paid, but I don't owe anything on it, and all my vendor bills are paid and up to date."

Binh stuck out her hand to shake Maile's. "Deal. I need a couple of days to get the gold bar for you."

"You know what? Don't give it to me." Maile got a business card from her bag. "This guy is my lawyer. His office is over on Fort Street. He has all the paperwork in there and knows I'm trying to unload…sell the place. Take the gold bar to him. I'll tell him to expect you this week. He'll know what to do."

"How're we going to sign paperwork?" Binh asked.

"Just sign your part in front of him. I'll come back here next week to sign everything else."

"What day? Because we can't really take walk-ins during holiday weekends."

Maile was short on time. "Are you open on Monday the First? Just think, you could be the proud owner of a new business on the first day of the year."

"Or the owner of the biggest flop ever." They both laughed. "I'll make time for you at noon."

***

When Christmas morning rolled around, Maile decided to sleep in. When she finally did leave for her mother's new place with Ka'uhane, it wasn't far away, well within walking distance. When she finally got there, the house was full of people, their wedding reception already under way. Brock had arrived after his late night patrol shift, and even Detective Ota was there, not too far from Maile's Aunt Kelani. While getting a tour of the house from her mother, and hearing all about the plans to spruce it up, they came across Susan Ota in the kitchen helping make a salad.

"You came with you dad?" Maile asked her.

"Kenny brought me. Is that okay?"

"Kenny?"

"Keneka brought Susan," Kealoha said, smiling approvingly at the girl.

Maile couldn't help but squint a little as she stared down her young employee, once her jailhouse nemesis. "Yes, this must be your second date with him?"

"Third, actually," Susan said, before quickly looking away.

Maile had a pretty good idea what that mean, but wasn't going there during a reception for her mother and new step-dad. She also wondered if Kenny was prepared for what was headed his way. "That's exciting."

"I'm dating your brother and my dad is dating your aunt. Pretty cool, huh?"

"Yeah, cool," Maile said, unsure if she meant it. Instead of hanging around the kitchen where she was at risk of being put to work peeling something, or hearing more gossip than what she was ready for, Maile excused herself with the message she was going to inspect the rest of the house. When she found her brother, it was in a bedroom that looked set up for his use. He was already using the Gameboy, playing a game of some sort. She went over to him and slapped his arm.

"Hey! What's that for?"

"For not telling me Mom was getting married yesterday!"

"She swore everybody to secrecy."

"From even telling me?"

"Especially from telling you. She didn't want you making a big fuss over it, which you know you would've."

"Of course I would've! She's our mom! How many times do we get so watch her get married?" Knowing it was a losing battle, she sat on the edge of the bed to watch the game his was playing. "What's the deal with Susan?"

"There's no deal."

"Are you dating for real? Because she thinks you guys are."

"Yes, and she's already told me all about her background, what she used to do, so you don't need to assassinate her character, or whatever."

"I wasn't going to. But you need to be aware of the fact that she's a lot more worldly than you."

"Worldly? What century are you from?"

"Shut up. Be careful with her."

"I'm not stupid, Maile."

"Maybe, maybe not. But Spencers ain't real bright when it comes to romance."

"Maybe you flopped, but Mom did okay marrying Reverend."

He had her there. "Just be careful with her. I know she looks good and knows how to talk real sweet with men, but don't get caught up in that."

"She doesn't treat me that way. We just hang out, doing stuff. I help her with her homework, and she's been helping me figure out a budget. She's pretty smart."

"I think she's very smart. What homework?"

"She's taking an algebra GED class in the evening. She's hoping to go to college next year, even."

Knowing Susan was busy working everyday as a tour guide, and taking classes in the evenings was a relief to Maile. There was only so much time Kenny and Susan could spend together before one of them had to be somewhere. "And if I hear that you've screwed that up for her, you better start running the next time I see you."

"When are you divulging your big news about where you're going?"

"Not today. It's not a Christmas thing. I'll tell Mom, and she can let everyone else know."

Maile went back to the living room to inspect the tree and its ornaments. Some were the ones she recognized from her childhood, mixed in with others that must've been Ka'uhane's. He was there, strumming his ukulele, the gift from Maile.

After a couple of songs, he joined her there at the tree. "You're quiet today, Hoku."

"Just a lot of things on my mind."

"About your mother marrying me and then moving in here?"

"That and a lot more. I guess I didn't like being tricked the way I was, with everybody keeping the wedding secret from me."

"It wouldn't have been such a secret if you'd had spent more time at home with your mother."

"Except that it's been years since that little cottage has been my home. Mom needs to understand that. You have a nice new house here, Reverend, but I can't move in here and pretend I'm a kid again, just so you and she can play house."

"We're not playing house, and we don't expect you to move in with us. Honestly, we'd rather you didn't. You and Keneka are always welcome to stay the night, but forget about moving in. What else is bothering you?"

"I'd rather not be counseled on Christmas Day."

"Since we're on the topic of withholding secrets, let me ask this. What are your plans for after the New Year holiday? You never have given us even a hint, only that you're going to the mainland to resume your nursing career."

"I need to tell Mom in person, and she'll be first. Otherwise, I don't want people trying to talk me out of it."

"It's honest work?" he asked.

"Of course. It's just that some people might not be open to the idea."

He led her to a sofa and sat with her. Others were on another sofa and easy chairs nearby, sipping cider or chatting about past Christmases. "You worry too much about other peoples' opinions of you, Hoku."

"Not much choice, is there?"

"All the choice in the world," he said.

"Maybe the most important thing you have to choose for yourself," her Aunt Kelani said, breaking into the conversation.

"I don't see how," Maile said. "Everything I do is scrutinized by others. Who I marry, where I live, how I spend my money, where I work, my friends, everything. Even the clothes I wear. As boring as my life has been the last year or so, it's been turned into a soap opera."

"Been anything but boring to watch," Kelani said, trying to hide her smile by taking a sip of cider.

"A lot of what you call a soap opera are the things that have worried the rest of us, Hoku."

"I know, Reverend. Everything is fine now. They weren't for a while, when things got a little chaotic, but my life is back on track."

"It's almost as if you forced things back on track, Maile," Kelani said. "Whether they needed to be or not."

Maile wanted that rum in her cider more than ever. "Maybe a little."

"Are you forcing yourself back on track, also?"

"What do you mean?"

Maybe because it was sounding like girltalk, the Reverend excused himself, leaving Maile and her aunt alone.

"I mean, you don't take to change very well. Sure, life has thrown you some curveballs lately, and you've somehow survived them mostly unscathed, but have you adapted to the changes in your life?"

"I…well…"

"Or do you keep going, revving your legs even faster, hoping to outrun change?"

Maile deflated the way a tire would on a car. "I don't know."

"Look at the way you took over your new tour company. You're still running it exactly the same way as your brother-in-law did. Same tours, same schedules, same old things."

"I have new employees. I just hired a new guide, and she's working out great. Plus, I have someone coming in to manage the business, and a new salesperson."

"I've heard about them. It's very nice of you to hire people who need the jobs, but will that take the business in a new direction, or keep doing the same old things the company has always done?"

"I've never been a businesswoman before, Auntie. I don't know about those things." Maile finished her cider and set the cup aside.

"When my husband and I were running our business, we were always looking for new ways to improve, to get new customers, to grow the business. I'm afraid your husband and brother-in-law never did that. That's what you've inherited from them, a business that is doomed to remain the same."

"It's in the black."

"But barely, from what your mother has told me. The point I'm trying to make isn't about how to run your business, but how you run yourself. If you can't control what's happening, you need to adapt to what's going on around you."

Maile studied her aunt for a moment. Kelani was very nearly a twin to her mother, except a slimmer, healthier woman, who wore updated clothing and had a sporty short hairstyle, while her mother looked much more traditionally Hawaiian, carrying a little too much weight beneath her muumuus, and having the old-fashioned braid in her hair that was coiled at the top of her head most of the time. While her aunt had taken the risk of selling the family home to make the move to Maui after her husband passed away, Maile's mother had clung to their little cottage with vice-like grips. It had taken a new husband to pry her out the door and into a new home. She'd even married a man who identified as Hawaiian. Maile could see then how much she was following in her mother's footsteps with how she conducted her life.

"I guess I don't want to lose my sense of being Hawaiian, even though I'm as much Japanese, white, and Samoan as I am Hawaiian."

"You won't," the Reverend said, sitting with them again. "You can be all of those things. You speak the language and practice the religion of white missionaries, which doesn't seem to upset you, or anyone else. You have many Japanese and Samoan friends, and often eat their foods."

"But I also believe in the ancient Hawaiian gods, even pray to them occasionally. I speak Hawaiian as well as I do English. It seems like everybody I know considers me Hawaiian before anything else."

"Because you do. And there's nothing wrong with that," Kelani said. "But I doubt you would go back to living the life of a native islander from before European contact, right? I know I sure wouldn't want to. I'll take sleeping in a bed instead of on a hala mat anytime."

When Ka'uhane laughed, Maile couldn't help laughing also. It reminded her of her recent run through the forest late at night, and how prickly nature was in the islands.

"Nope. Indoor plumbing and electricity is pretty nice, too."

"It's almost as if you're dedicated to being known Hawaiian and nothing but," Kelani said. "Look Hawaiian, speak Hawaiian, eat Hawaiian food. I've seen that little apartment of yours. That's not much better than living in a hut made from sticks at the beach."

"The beach would be an upgrade from that place," Maile muttered.

Maile excused herself to get more cider, and decided she'd had enough self-improvement for one day. When she found Brock, his eyes were barely open. She knew then it wasn't the right time to give him the special gift she had, and instead gave him the box with a necktie. Walking him out to his pickup, she watched as he climbed in.

"You can stay awake till you get home?"

"It's only a few blocks."

She kept him from closing the door. "I don't want you dying. Not now."

"What's so important about now that I can't die versus any other time?"

She leaned into the cab of the pickup, took his face in her hands, and kissed him.

"Because I love you now."

Chapter Seventeen

When Monday morning rolled around, Maile felt like she had a Christmas hangover. There had been too much food, too much cider, too much gossip, and now she was suffering the consequences. The magnitude of that would surely show up before the end of the week with even more gossip about her being spread around.

Not only were Brian and Amelia already at the Manoa Tour office when Maile got there, but Susan was also.

"Talk to my dad?" Susan asked as they went into the office.

"Not since yesterday."

"He said he was going to call you about something."

"What about?"

"I don't know. He was crabby, which means it was about something official."

"Great," Maile mumbled as she sat at her desk. "Just what I need is another police investigation that involves me, and a grumpy detective in charge of it."

No sooner were they seated at desks logging onto computers, that Lopaka, Danny, and Christy showed up. Lopaka was as cheerful as always, Danny sat in a corner waiting for his driving assignment for the day, but Christy looked hungover for real. Once the tour guides and their drivers went out, Maile set her attention on finding advertising for her little company. After her long talks with Reverend Ka'uhana and her Aunt Kelani the day before, she had decided to turn over a new leaf with trying to grow her business, even if she was running out of time to accomplish much.

"We have ideas about that, Maile," Amelia said. "Brian, show her the mock-ups of the flyers you made."

Maile was impressed with the creativity of the trifold brochures he'd created, the type of thing that could be found in airport terminals and hotel lobbies. They also discussed what could be done with internet advertising, and Maile reluctantly gave Brian a budget to spend on it. With the warning to them to not waste too much time on advertising and focus on sales calls, she left the office with the thumb drive that contained the ad brochures to be printed. Walking to a print shop a few blocks away, she got a call from Detective Ota.

"There's news about Oscar Swenberg," he said.

"He's run off again? Skipped out on paying his bill at the hospice, too?"

"In a way. He died last died in his sleep."

"Oh." That hit pretty hard, and somehow she needed to find a way of apologizing for her crass remarks, but to whom? "He didn't look long for the world when I visited the other day. I hope he went gently. But what does that have to do with me?"

"It seems to have been a family thing. Laurie Long passed last night, also."

"What?" Maile got to the bench at a bus stop so she could sit down. "Laurie died? Wait. Which Laurie Long?"

"You one you saw hooked up to the breathing machine a while back, the real Laurie Long."

"Does her family know?"

"They would've been notified by the rehab center. Oscar and Laurie died within an hour of each other. Strange, since they hadn't seen each other in months and were at opposite ends of town. I suppose the rehab center has already contacted the Longs. The only reason I know is because I still had open investigations going on both of them, and the Swenberg brothers, and both facilities had to inform me if and when they ever passed. Those calls came in the middle of the night."

"I guess that means your Swenberg investigations are now closed?" Maile asked.

"Mostly. Honey is still out there. I'd like to talk with her for a few minutes, just to get some clarity on all the various relationships between Laurie, Honey, and the three Swenberg brothers. There's something very peculiar going on with them that I just can't put a finger on."

"If you ever figure it out, let me know," she said.

"That's the important thing to you, isn't it? To know what makes someone tick?" he asked.

Maile chuckled. "Drives me nuts when I don't."

Once she was done at the printer, Maile called the office to check on things there. Making the excuse she was going to make a few in-person sales calls, she took the rest of the morning off. Her first stop was at a flower shop she and her mother frequented, one owned by an acquaintance, Binh Nghiem.

When Maile wasn't able to make her needs known to the Vietnamese woman working in the front of the store, Binh was called from a back room. As usual, her large eyes and glossy hair caught Maile's attention, and even wearing a grubby apron over her clothes, the young woman was an eyeful.

"If you're wondering about the gold bar for a dive bar deal, I'm going to see your lawyer later today," Binh said, still arranging some flowers.

"Actually, I came in for a bouquet of flowers."

"Your mother usually comes in on Fridays for your church flowers."

"These are for friends who've lost a family member. They're Chinese. Any idea of what sort of flowers are appropriate to take them?"

"If they're Buddhist, pretty much the same as for the Vietnamese," Binh said. She went to a cooler to collect cut flowers. "To you Christians, white lilies mean purity and love, but to us, white is used to represent death instead of black, and lilies are thought of as being gentle. Having white lilies at a funeral is a way of gently sending the person's soul off to its next life, wishing it well. I'll give you eight, which is an auspicious number for us."

"Why auspicious?" Maile asked, watching as the girl went about making the arrangement.

"Even numbers tend to represent negative things, but the number eight is a good luck number in Asian cultures. It's sort of a way to integrate both the mourning of the death and the happiness of them finding a new life to live."

"Wow. You guys put a lot of thought into things."

"We're kinda superstitious when it comes to death, birth, and moving into new places to live or work."

"I just want a bunch of cheerful, colorful flowers."

"Which might've insulted your Chinese friends. I went to your bar yesterday, by the way. That place is a dud."

"You want to back out of our deal?" Maile asked.

"We think we can make something of it. All that British pub stuff is going in the dumpster, though. Whose idea was that?"

"My ex-husband. He had a lot of dud ideas."

"What's the deal with that bartender?" Binh asked.

"Ace? Nothing. Why?"

"Didn't like the looks of me or my aunties, that's for sure."

"Oh. He's a Vietnam War vet. Maybe he still has a few ill feelings."

Binh wrapped the bouquet in plastic wrap. "If he wants to keep his job, he'll need to get over it. If we buy the place, we plan to earn money, and that means everybody will need to get along, whether we like the looks of each other or not."

"I think if you gave him a case of beer and a fistful of cash, he'd retire."

Maile got her flowers for free, just like everything else she got from Binh and her businesses. She wasn't sure how many cultural rules she was breaking when she knocked on the front door of the Long house in central Honolulu, but she was going to pay her sympathies.

The brother came to the door, with Laurie's little girl hiding behind him, peeking from around his leg. She seemed more interested in the flowers than in Maile.

"You came back," he said. "We didn't think you'd ever return. None of Laurie's other social workers ever came back a second time."

"Hi. I heard she passed away last night. I came to offer my condolences." She stuck the bouquet out in front of her.

"Who is it?" a woman called from inside the house.

"That social worked came back."

"Which one?"

"The one that was here last week."

Maile heard footsteps pad through the house and a door slam. A moment later, Laurie's mother came to the door. Her eyes were red as though she'd been crying, her hair disheveled, and her face not made up like the first time Maile had met her. She looked back and forth between the flowers and at Maile's face.

"Laurie…is not here. I told you that the last time you came."

"I know she's been in that rehab center, and that she passed away last night. I'm very sorry to hear about that." She tried again handing over the flowers to anyone that might take them. "I just want to offer my condolences."

"Baby, take the flowers from the lady," the woman said to the little girl, still hiding.

She slowly eased from around the young man and took the bouquet in both hands. With that, she was led away to the kitchen by her young uncle. Mrs. Long swung the door open wider.

"You may as well come in. Please pardon the mess." Maile kicked off her shoes and followed Mrs. Long into the small living room. The host called out for something in Chinese, and then smiled at Maile. "My mother will bring us tea."

"I don't mean to spend so much time. Maybe I should go?"

"You're a welcome distraction from everything else. And thank you for the flowers. Very considerate."

Granny Long, as she was being called, brought a tray with three cups and a pot of aromatic tea, muttering about something. Mrs. Long poured cups for each of them after Granny sat next to Maile on the small sofa. Of everyone in the house, she looked the most distraught.

"Please tell Granny how sorry I am about her granddaughter passing."

"She already knows, and thanks you for the flowers."

"Please understand I would come to the funeral, but I'm leaving town soon."

"Why would a social worker come to a funeral?" Mrs. Long asked.

"I'm not a social worker, just a friend of her and Oscar."

"Oh yes, him. At least with my daughter gone, he's now out of our lives forever."

Maile finished the small cup of tea and set it aside. "I guess you don't know. Oscar has also passed away."

Mrs. Long looked genuinely stunned. "I knew he wasn't well. Not sorry hearing about him, though."

"I spoke with him recently. He was planning to leave everything to Laurie, to pay for the expenses of her living in rehab. I'm sure you'll hear from his lawyer soon about his will."

"To Laurie? We've been expecting it to go to that other…to Honey."

The little girl showed up again, carrying the vase of flowers Maile had brought. All three women watched as she carefully put it on the small coffee table and pushed it to the middle. After that, she looked at each woman in turn, and silently decided to sit on Maile's lap. She learned the girl's name was Clarice. With that, Granny left them alone.

"From what I understand. Oscar passed before Laurie did, so she should still be able to receive the inheritance," Maile said. "Or you would now, I suppose. I'm sorry, I shouldn't have brought all this up."

"We need to deal with it eventually. These things are good to know. I'm not sure I trust Oscar's lawyer any more than I did him."

Clarice squirmed on Maile's lap when Granny brought another tray in, this one stacked high with wet, steaming bamboo baskets. When the scent of damp bamboo and steamed food hit Maile's nose, she realized she was hungrier than she thought.

Small doughy buns were loaded onto plates and handed around along with chopsticks, Clarice using her fingers to take a bite from one of them.

"I wasn't expecting a meal," Maile said, wondering what to do with the chopsticks and food.

"You don't realize you've stumbled into a Buddhist way of mourning," Mrs. Long said. "We generally have a three week period before the funeral during which we receive old friends and family who want to offer their condolences. It would be impolite for us not to offer a little something to make the moment easier. Please, enjoy."

With a mental shrug of her shoulders, Maile jabbed the tips of her chopsticks into the soft bun on her plate. She heard a slight gasp from Granny, and Mrs. Long shifted on her chair nervously. When Clarice noticed what Maile had done, she pulled the bun loose from the chopsticks and arranged the tips of the sticks on either side on the bun.

"Like that," she mewed softly.

"Sorry."

The brother joined them, and ten minutes later, they were done with the simple meal.

"These were delicious, Mrs. Long."

"Granny's recipe from the old country. She's very picky about ingredients. She taught me, and she taught Laurie…"

Granny interrupted her daughter, and the two of them went to the kitchen for what sounded like a spat in Chinese.

"My grandmother knows more English than what my mother realizes," the boy said to Maile.

"I really have interrupted your home on a sad day."

"Not so sad as it might seem. I think we said goodbye to Laurie a long time ago. All except Granny. She had some weird idea Laurie was coming home someday."

Maile listened as more words were exchanged and doors were slammed in the house. At one point, it sounded like a third voice joined the argument. When neither Mrs. Long nor Granny returned, Maile knew it was time to go. Just as she was leaving the front door, she heard another door slam at the back of the house, as though someone else was leaving at the same time.

"That was the worst idea ever," Maile said as she walked along in the sunshine. "What kind of dope am I to drop in on a family like that?"

When she got to the end of the block, she noticed someone coming from the alley behind the row of houses. She was wearing a long dress and a large hat, and seemed to be in a hurry. It wasn't Mrs. Long; the figure was wrong and the clothes too young. The long ponytail that hung down seemed familiar with blond highlights in it.

"That's Honey," she mumbled, stepping up her pace. "I'd know that figure from a mile away."

She kept pace with Honey from half a block back, and didn't seem to get noticed. Once they were to busier streets, Maile caught up a little, just to make sure she didn't lose her to a bus or shop. When she saw Honey go into a sailor's bar, Maile went to the front door but stalled. Looking in, the place was mostly empty, except a couple of tables with one man each nursing a broken heart or lost career, whatever parts of their souls men pacify in bars.

She spotted Honey seated at the bar, not working in the place. She decided to go in and took the seat next to her.

"You followed me," Honey said more as a statement than as a question.

"You were at the house when I was there, weren't you?"

"So what if I was?"

"And you know about Laurie?"

"Duh. Half the Chinese people in town already know she'd dead."

"You could be a little more soft-hearted about it," Maile said. She ignored the iced tea that she'd ordered.

"Be a soft-hearted sap like you? Forget that. I want my share of the money, which is all of it."

"What makes you think you get any of it? From what I've heard, you and Oscar weren't even married."

"You really are an idiot, you know that?" Honey said.

"Hey, I'm not the one trying to weasel her way into someone else's inheritance. Good luck with that. And I can tell you're really broken-hearted about Oscar dying last night," Maile said sarcastically.

Honey stirred her golden drink with the plastic swizzle stick. "You don't know what I'm feeling right now."

"I know you spent several weeks in alcohol treatment on Oscar's dime, and now you're hitting the sauce again."

"Is that why you followed me? To harass me?"

"No. I just want to know why you continue to hang around with the Longs when you know full well they don't want you there."

Honey looked at Maile with wet eyes. "To be with my daughter, okay? As soon as we get our share of the inheritance, the Longs' can kiss our rear ends goodbye."

"Your daughter?"

"Duh, like hello? Clarice is my daughter, not Laurie's."

"Stop talking to me that way. Mrs. Long told me Clarice is Laurie's daughter."

"That's what they want to believe. That old granny back there wants to adopt her as theirs. Who do they think they are, trying to adopt my daughter?"

"Maybe because she lives with them and they're raising her? She's not completely Chinese. Who's her father, anyway? Oscar?"

Honey stirred the ice cubes in her drink again. "Does it matter?"

"I think it matters to whoever raises her."

They sat quietly, Honey stirring her drink, Maile staring at the iced tea she had no interest in.

"I don't know, okay?"

"How can you not…never mind."

"You don't get out much, do you?"

"Apparently not," Maile said. "It's not Oscar?"

Honey snorted a laugh through her nose. "Oscar was no more capable of fathering a child than I am."

"He wasn't that old. Clarice would've been born long before he'd been injured by those gangsters a while back."

"Let me put it this way. Oscar didn't have the wherewithal to be a father. Get it?"

"I'm confused," Maile said.

"Oscar was gay. Believe me, because I tried my best to make something happen, and I know Laurie did too."

"Gay? I never picked up on that with him."

"Oh, he wasn't flaming on fire, but he had his secret little rendezvous from time to time."

"He was married to Laurie, and you lived with him. How could he be gay?" Maile asked.

Honey snorted derisively again. "You and those Longs back there, sitting around passing judgment over me wanting my share of the inheritance. What a joke."

"Why?"

"Laurie was as big of a fraud as Oscar was. Or me, for that matter. All she wanted from him was an easy lifestyle, big houses, and an endless expense allowance. He handed out money to her and me like allowances for little kids."

"So, even after you knew he was gay, both of you continued to stick it out with him?"

"The money was good. Who wouldn't stay with him?" Honey continued to play with the drink instead of drink it. "Eventually, Laurie came back here to Honolulu, and got a little too stoned at a party. That's when she ended up in that rehab place."

"I'm still not convinced you're Clarice's mother and Laurie isn't," Maile said.

"Okay, which one of us is built like a mother? Who has hips that have given birth and has breasts that have fed a baby?"

Maile didn't need to look at Honey's figure to know the answer to that. "But if Oscar isn't the father, who is?"

"One of his brothers. Or maybe an actor. My agent and the producer to those movies had me so stoned most of the time, I didn't know the difference between making one of their smut movies and the real thing."

Maile was confused again. "I thought it was Laurie that was making those pornos?"

"She was, until she was a little too unreliable with the booze she was drinking."

"Unreliable as in…?"

"Right. She was too drunk to get into the scenes in the way they needed her to. So, Oscar sent me to finish out her contract. When I got there, I needed to step in and finish a movie where she'd left off. They just needed to fix my hair and dabble with the makeup, and I was a dead ringer for Laurie. A few weeks later, I was pregnant and needed to go to rehab to get off the stuff they'd been feeding me. That was the first of three times."

"And all you and Laurie ever really wanted was to live in a nice house and have lots of money, but both of you ended up in rehab. Eventually, Laurie died, and you have a daughter that's being passed back and forth between you and the family raising her."

Honey finally pushed her drink away, untouched. "Glad you asked?"

"Not really." Maile put enough money on the bar to pay for her iced tea, also untouched. She stood from the barstool and set it back in place. "Good luck in getting your share of the inheritance."

"Just so you know, those tears you saw on Mrs. Long weren't exactly the tears of a broken heart. She and Granny are already talking about how to spend the money."

"Oh yeah?"

"They're thinking of opening a restaurant. They should thank Laurie for that, but I doubt they will."

When Maile left the bar, she called Detective Ota back.

"Don't worry about Honey, Detective. She's not doing anything illegal. Immoral maybe, but not illegal."

"How do you know?" he asked.

"I just got through talking with her." She explained the story as best she could without making any of them look too guilty. "If anybody needs investigating, it would be Laurie's mother. She's a little too sneaky for her own good."

***

When Maile got home at the end of the day, the door to the Mendoza's old apartment hung open. Unable to control her curiosity, Maile peeked in. Mrs. Taniguchi was there, filling out forms. The small apartment had gotten a fresh coat of paint and new carpeting had been put down. Even the windows that looked out at the street were clean.

"It's nice in here, Mrs. Taniguchi."

"Too late if you want to move in, Maile. It's already rented."

"I'm moving out of my place next Monday, remember?"

That got the attention of the elderly landlady. "You are?"

"I gave you all the paperwork, and even a reminder notice on your door."

"That was from you?"

"You don't remember?"

Mrs. Taniguchi went past Maile to her room across the hall and waited to be let in. Once she was, she looked around as if she were thinking of moving in. "All this stuff belongs to the apartment?"

"What stuff? I never had much in here except my clothes and a few kitchen things."

"What about the fan?" Mrs. Taniguchi asked.

Maile laughed at the memory of the trouble with the fan. "Whoever moves in next can have that stupid thing."

"What day do you move out?"

"Monday the First. First thing in the morning."

"That's when the new girl moves in across the hall. Nice girl. You'd like her. Good job. Reliable."

"Maybe she'll want my fan?"

"Not if I get to it first," Mrs. Taniguchi said.

***

Maile's most difficult task in preparation for leaving town came on Sunday, New Year's Eve morning. She was due to meet Brock later in the day to spend the day—and night—together one last time before she left town on Tuesday. As it was, she'd been spending more time at his cottage that week than in her little room. When the time came, Maile got a bath towel and went out to King's aviary at the back of the house near the garden. When she went inside, it wasn't to fill his food or water bowls, or to scrape his perches or floor clean. He followed, hopping along the ground as she went to the backyard. Once he was there, she watched closely as he rummaged through flowerbeds filled with vines, looking for bugs and fresh food. Once he'd had his fill, she wrapped him in the bath towel and went off down the street to the pet and feed store.

"Time for his wings to be clipped, Kamalei."

The storeowner, long a friend of Maile, held out his hand for King to climb onto. "Be glad to. It'll take me just a few minutes, if you wouldn't mind watching the store."

Maile went straight to the large parrot that spent most of its time at the cash register. After giving it a peanut to disassemble, she stroked his chest with a fingertip. "I'll need a large bag of seed, also."

"I heard you're leaving town soon?" Kamalei called from where he was working on King's wings.

"Day after tomorrow."

"Who's going to take care of your little buddy?"

"King is on his way to a bird farm out in Waimanalo. I've been talking to the owner of the place, and even went out there to visit the other day. I think it's time for King to retire and talk to birds instead of humans."

"I know that place. Good set-up. He'll be happy out there. Plenty of space to fly around and trees to sit in."

"They don't fly away?" she asked. "I'm worried he'll come back here looking for me."

"I doubt it." Kamalei brought King back to Maile, the job done. "I happen to know there are a couple of wahine cockatiels out there. I'm sure they'll catch his eye."

She rubbed King's face. "Hear that? You'll have your own little harem."

It was a long bus ride for them both, across town and partway around the island to get to the bird farm. When each new passenger got on, they looked at King perched on Maile's hand, the large bag of seed on the seat next to her. When one guy got a little too clever with his antics with her and King, she lifted him quickly enough so he flapped his wings.

"He's not just my pet, he's my bodyguard."

"I'm supposed to be afraid of a bird?"

"Only when he starts to rip out your eyeballs with his beak."

When she got off the bus, it was a long walk up a double-track driveway. Tall trees grew here and there, with lower levels of trees and shrubs everywhere. King perked up when there was the call of large birds.

"Oh, you like that, don't you? You'll finally have someone intelligent to talk to."

Maile walked slower and slower the closer she got to the entrance of the bird sanctuary, taking a few minutes to think of their lives together. Once she was in, she handed over the bag of seed to a helper and found the man who ran the place.

"This is King?" he asked. "I know him. He was here just a couple of weeks ago."

"Yeah, he flew off for a few days. I thought I'd lost him forever that time."

"His wings clipped like I asked?"

"Yep. Just had it done." She gave him the envelope of cash she'd promised to bring.

"I like it to be done so they can't fly back to where they used to live right away. This way, he'll get to know his way around here, make a few friends, and hopefully forget all about you by the time his wings grow in again."

"I hope he doesn't forget me completely."

"When he was here a while back, he was quite taken with the two lady cockatiels we have here. They've been nesting ever since."

"Where should I put him?" Maile asked hesitantly.

"Over in the vines below that monkey pod tree. He already knows that tree."

Maile looked up into the broad tree and saw two white cockatiels on heavy branches looking down at them. One let out a screech as though it was calling for King to join them.

"He'll be able to get up there with clipped wings?"

The man laughed. "He's got two wahine waiting for him. He'll find a way."

Maile took King over to an area overgrown with vines and shrubs. Having a hard time keeping her eyes dry, she rubbed his face for the last time. "Okay, friend. You behave yourself out here. This is a nice place. And you act like a gentleman around those wahine, understand?"

He bobbed his head up and down as though he understood.

"Not too much of a gentleman, though."

She swung her arm into the air and King leapt to the ground. Almost immediately, he hopped to the vines and climbed inside, looking for an easy meal. When she backed away, she stood at the far end of the farm, watching him for a while. It didn't take long before he found a way of climbing the tall monkey pod, joining his new friends on a branch. Almost immediately, they began preening each other.

"Just like old friends," the man said, also watching.

Maile smiled in spite of her tears. "Yep, just like old friends."

***

"What's wrong with you?" Brock asked at dinner that evening. Somehow, he'd been able to reserve a table in a restaurant that overlooked Waikiki Beach for their New Year's dinner.

"Sorry I'm so mopey. Just thinking about stuff."

"About going to the mainland in a couple of days? You don't have to go. Just call them and back out politely."

"I wish it were so easy as that."

"You are eventually telling me where you're going, right?"

She smiled. "Tomorrow evening, I promise. But I need to tell my mom first."

"Just so you know, I'm holding you down to the floor and tickling you until you tell me."

She laughed. "I'll need something like that to cheer me up tomorrow."

"What else is bothering you?" he asked.

"Oh, taking King to the farm today, saying goodbye to the Mendozas, giving up my little apartment, Mom moving out of the cottage. Just everything changing at once."

"You hate that dump. How could anyone ever miss that crummy little room you lived in?"

"I know. I was the only place I've ever called my own. I went from living with Mom to moving in with Robbie. As junky as the place is, it was mine."

"Noisy, hot, crowded, and you never seemed to have any food in the place. Except those little doughnuts. What is it with you and doughnuts?" he asked.

"Comfort food." Maile thought about how she'd probably not get any for a while, or poi, and knew exactly where to go the get some that evening. "See you at the beach later? Promise to show up?"

"There'll be a lot of people there. How will I find you?"

"Look for the girl that's not a tourist."

***

Brock had a day shift to work on New Year's Day and needed to leave Maile's little apartment early. She had only three errands to run that day before meeting Brock again later in the afternoon at Waikiki Beach. When she left her little apartment for the last time, she needed to hand off her set of keys to Mrs. Taniguchi. That wasn't going to be difficult, since she was out in the hallway watching the new tenant move into the Mendoza's old place.

Maile listened to whoever it was inside the little apartment putting things away as she gave the elderly landlady her keys. "Is it a guy or girl moving in?"

"Nice Japanese girl. Young thing. I wish all the kids these days could be as nice as this one. I thought they broke the mold when they made you, Maile."

"You think I'm nice? We've had words with each other."

"Always honest when you had your words with me. Can't blame you for that."

That's when the new tenant came back to where Maile and Mrs. Taniguchi were talking. Maile got what she hoped was her only surprise of the day.

"What're you doing here?" Susan Ota asked, looking as confused as Maile felt.

"You're the one moving in?"

"Yeah. You don't have to check on me, or where I live."

"I'm not. I'm moving out of that place," Maile said, pointing at her recently vacated room. "What happened to your hair?"

Susan ran her fingers through her hair. She'd gotten a trim to her already short style, but it was also now blond. "Starting the new year with something different. Think my boss will mind?"

Maile smiled politely. "I think it should be okay." She noticed the confusion on Mrs. Taniguchi's face. "Susan works at the tour company I own. She's my newest guide."

"No problem making rent payments, then," the woman said.

Maile offered the little bit of kitchen stuff she had, along with the fan, to Susan. Maile watched for a moment while Susan decided where to put things. When Mrs. Taniguchi started a conversation with Susan in Japanese, Maile left them alone to figure out the new set of rules Susan would need to follow. She also figured living under Mrs. Taniguchi's roof wouldn't be any easier for Susan than living under her father's.

***

Her first errand took her to the airport to leave brochures for her tour company in the tourist activities rack near entrances. After filling several racks, she went to the place she needed to find in the departures terminal early the next morning.

After leaving the airport, she called Brian, Amelia, Susan, Lopaka, Danny, and Christy to check with each of them about their jobs going forward. She left Lopaka for last.

"Your New Year's bonus is in Brian's desk drawer. Don't start comparing because you got a little extra, brah."

"You're really leaving us? Can't convince you to stay?"

"Sorry. I wish people wouldn't keep asking. It just makes it harder."

"Tell me where you're going and I'll stop."

"It's all explained on a note inside the bonus envelope."

"Just tell me, Mai."

"Okay, fine." She explained to him her plans and why she needed to leave town. "Keep it to yourself, okay? I need to tell Brock in my own way."

He laughed. "Yeah, and I heard that way is fun, too!"

After that came the trip to Reverend Ka'uhane's house to see her mother.

"The first thing we need to straighten out, Hoku," he said. "Is that you can't keep calling me Reverend Ka'uhane."

"I might be a little old to think of you as my dad."

"Ka'uhane should be fine. I'm retired from the ministry now. No need for formalities."

"I'll try. It might take me a while, but I'll try. Can I talk to my mom alone for a few minutes, please?"

Her mother poured two glasses of mango juice and sat at the kitchen table with Maile. "Okay, for the last time Maile girl, what's this big secret job you have? Going to work for the CIA?"

"Ha! It would almost be easier to tell you about that." It went easier than Maile had expected and got very little resistance from her mother, leaving her to think it wasn't as big of a deal as they'd been thinking.

"You'll be good at that," Kealoha said.

"I can't believe I'll be so far away. "I'll miss you so much. All my life, you've always been right here on the same island."

"I always thought you'd move into the cottage when I finally moved out."

"I never thought you'd move out!"

"Get enough incentive and a person will do anything. Good that Brock moved in. He still likes it there?" Kealoha asked.

"Seems like it. He has more space and can live alone again."

"Not so alone this last week, from what I hear from the neighbors."

"Oh, you've heard I've been spending the nights there with him."

"No shame in that, Maile girl. Not with Ka'uhane, either. The bigger shame would've been if you hadn't. You two meant for each other."

"You think so?"

"Been thinking that since you two were keiki."

Maile rummaged through her bag for a small box that she gave to her mother. "I got this for him. You think it's okay?"

Kealoha opened the box and smiled when she saw what was inside. "A gold ring? It's pretty. For him to wear?"

"If he wants to."

"Proposing marriage?"

"Not exactly that. Just making a promise."

"Does it mean you're coming back here someday?" Kealoha asked.

"Of course. This is my home. Everybody I know is here. Where else would I go?"

"Maybe find another kane to be with?" her mother asked.

"You know how you said that you've known since we were keiki that Brock and I belong together? Well, so have I. I just made the mistake of finding another kane to waste my time with."

Kealoha gave the ring box back. "Not a waste of time if you learned your lesson."

"What lesson is that?" Maile asked.

"That you and Brock belong together."

***

Maile had one last errand to do before returning to Waikiki, and since it was early, she had plenty of time for it. As she road along on the bus, watching the same familiar sights she'd seen a hundred times, she got a call from Detective Ota.

"My last day off before I leave town tomorrow, Detective. I don't feel like going on any stakeouts with you."

"What about with Turner?" he asked.

"Looking for gossip? Because you should be able to get plenty of that from your daughter these days."

He laughed. "No, I just need to you come to the station."

Maile was already within walking distance of the police station. "Now? I have things to do."

"It shouldn't take long."

"If it's about some murder somewhere, I had nothing to do with it."

"Feeling pretty defensive about something?" he asked.

"Look, every murder, every crime, everything culprit that you've tried to associate with me in the last year has gone nowhere. You have to admit, once and for all, I'm clean."

"Except for one little matter. Come to the station so we can talk about it."

Maile yanked on the cord to ring the bell to be let off the bus. Walking back a block, she went inside the small lobby where she was met by an officer who seemed to be waiting for her.

"You know what this is all about?" she asked him.

"No, Ma'am. Detective Ota just needs to talk to you about something important. He said no matter what, not you let you lout of my sight."

"That's not very reassuring."

When Maile got to Ota's desk, he was standing there, along with two other officers. He pretended to get busy with something, and ignored the cop that spoke to Maile.

"Miss Maile Spencer?"

"Yes, but I wish you guys would call me Ms. Spencer or just Maile."

"Ma'am, turn around please, and put your hands behind your back."

"Huh?"

"Do as he says, Ms. Spencer and this will go a lot easier for all of us," Ota said, now watching.

Maile turned a little and put her wrists together behind her back. "What's going on? Why are you doing this?"

Ota picked up a stack of white slips from his desk. "I have here several unpaid parking and traffic citations, all of which are months overdue. In fact, here's one from two years ago."

She looked at the array of citations in his hand. "I forgot all about those."

"Did HPD Officer Brock Turner talk to you about paying these?"

"Well, yes, but…"

"But they're still unpaid, is that correct?"

"Yes."

"And you have the means to pay them?"

He had her there. She even told Ota about the settlement from the hospital that had been deposited to her bank account. "Yes."

"Then we need to place you under arrest until a court date can be arranged."

"A court date? I'm leaving town tomorrow!"

"Take her to Interrogation Room One," Ota told the officer.

When she went in, a man in a suit sat behind the metal desk that was bolted to the floor. The officer carefully settled Maile into a chair across from him. "I'm sorry, I don't know what's going on here," she said.

"My name is Judge Wilson. The station commander has asked me to come here today to take care of this matter of parking and traffic citations."

"This is a hearing? Because I don't have the money with me to pay whatever fine …" Maile thought of her date with Brock later, and how she was going to miss their last night together. "…and I can't possibly spend time in jail."

"I'll manage this session, thank you."

Maile looked around and saw what must've been a dozen cops and detectives watching, Ota right in the middle of them. He was as grim-faced as all the rest of them, and the judge.

"For the record, state your full legal name," the judge said, pen in hand, jotting notes on a yellow pad.

"Hokuhoku'ikalani Spencer."

The judge picked up the traffic tickets. "These all have the name Maile Spencer on them."

"Usually I go by…"

Detective Ota interrupted. "I can attest her correct name is Hokuhoku'ikalani Spencer."

The judge made a few notes on his pad, and then looked at the parking tickets. "Do you own an orange Hyundai two-door subcompact?"

"I just…"

Again, Ota interrupted by handing over a sheet of paper to the judge. "That vehicle belongs to A-1 Towing and Wrecking, your Honor."

Maile looked up at Ota. "But…"

He shook his head for her to be quiet.

The judge flipped through the tickets again. "Detective, there seems to be some irregularities in this matter. The defendant's name does not match what is on the citations, and she does not own the car described in these parking tickets. Do you have an explanation for that?"

"No, your Honor, I don't."

Maile watched as the judge filled out a form and signed the bottom.

"Thank you for your cooperation, Ms. Spencer. Please rise for sentencing."

The officer that had taken her in there asked her to stand.

"What's going on?" she asked, once she was on her feet.

"Ms. Spencer, I sentence you to the fullest extent the law allows, which is a fine and jail time."

"Why? Just for some stupid tickets? I have to be somewhere tomorrow morning!"

"I'm afraid your sentence is for longer than that," the judge said. "At least until such time as you can pay your fine."

"What? Detective Ota, call my mother. Or just call Brock. He'll pay it!"

"Detective, do you see any reason for me to suspend her sentence?"

"No, your Honor. Because of her recidivist behavior, I think she should pay the fine and spend the time in jail."

"Recidivist behavior? They're parking tickets! Okay, fine, there are a couple of speeding tickets. So what? I bet there are hundreds of people out there with more tickets than that!"

The judge looked around at the gathering of officers and detectives. "Ladies and gentlemen, as a jury of her peers, what say you?"

"Double the fine," someone said.

"Month in county lockup," another mentioned.

"What?"

"I can go to the hardware store for lumber to build a gallows in the parking lot," one last man said.

That voice was familiar. When Maile turned around, Brock was standing in the middle, grinning. That's when she noticed all the rest of them were grinning, some beginning to laugh.

"What's going on?" she asked again.

Ota stepped forward and took the cuffs from off her wrists. "Just having one last bit of police station fun with you, Maile."

"Was this real?" She looked at the man behind the table, now putting a few things away in her briefcase. Even he was smiling as he handed over the citation to a clerk to shred. "Are you really a judge?"

"Meet Judge Joe Wilson, retired judge from the Honolulu municipal court system," Ota said. "He comes in to do a few favors for us from time to time. Today, you were our guest."

Judge Wilson smiled and shook Maile's hand. "Just so you know, the forms and verdict of not guilty for lack of evidence is binding and will be filed as such. Good luck on your upcoming ventures, Miss."

After the judge was gone and the others had wandered off, Maile glared at Brock and Ota. "You know, the two of you really are a pair of…"

"Care to take a tour of the cell block?" Ota asked, interrupting. "Some of your old friends are in there."

"Not my friends. May I go?"

Brock walked Maile out to the sidewalk, and gave her the quickest of pecks to her cheek. "Mad?"

She playing punched him in the belly. "I'm not the only one with surprises up their sleeve."

Instead of taking the bus for the rest of her journey, she decided to walk through downtown, past the Iolani Palace, and into Chinatown. She was hoping to find Binh at the Vietnamese pho diner to check on the status of the 'bar for a bar' deal, as it had come to be called whenever they talked on the phone that week. The diner was packed full of patrons, all of them having large bowls of dumplings or noodles. Red sheets of paper with the same Chinese character were taped or glued to every window, door, and wall in the place.

"Binh at salon," one of the waitresses said.

Maile walked to the next shop down, and it too was busy with patrons having hair and nails done. Binh was just finishing one lady's nails when Maile went in.

"Got all the paperwork signed," she said to Maile at the cash register. She popped open the register drawer, lifted the coin tray, and took out a stack of legal paperwork. Binh tapped a glossy fingernail on the top sheet. "Your friend David put these little stickies everywhere you need to sign."

Maile took the pen that was given to her. She pressed the pen tip to the paper, but hesitated.

"Chickening out?" Binh asked.

"No. He accepted the gold bar as payment in full?"

"He said he talked to you and you said it was okay. If it's okay with you, it's okay with me."

Maile carefully read every page twice. Not seeing any loopholes or anything to call her lawyer about, she signed everything. Slapping down the pen, she shook Binh's hand.

"Good luck with the bar."

"Thanks. We already have big ideas for the place."

"Good. My biggest idea was to get rid of it as fast as I could." Maile looked at the two stylists working on hair, and the women waiting in chairs. "Looks like you don't have time for me?"

"For hair? Are you nuts? Today and Lunar New Years are the two biggest days of the year. Everybody wants to start the New Year with a new style, or a facial, or nails, anything that makes them look pretty. Totally superstitious about that."

"Just like with the flowers I gave someone a few days ago?"

"Exactly. Did you see all those people in the diner next door? What were they eating?"

"Dumplings and noodles," Maile said.

"Okay, more superstition. Dumplings are called 'wrapped babies' in Asian languages, which is a New Year thing, right? And we eat only full-length noodles on New Year's Day, so it'll be a long and prosperous year."

"That's interesting. Maybe I should go back and have a small bowl of each?"

"Better to have a big bowl of each. What do you want to do with your hair?"

Maile dug a picture out of her bag and showed it to Binh.

"Big change. That's right, you're leaving town soon, aren't you? Good time for a change. No one at the new place will know anything's different about you."

"What do you mean?" Maile asked.

"You know, in case something goes wrong."

That didn't offer the reassurance Maile needed right then. "I leave tomorrow morning. I guess I shouldn't have put this off for so long."

"Perfect day for it." Binh looped her arm through Maile's to hold her there. "My two regular stylists are booked up for the rest of the day, but I have a new girl that nobody trusts yet. Instead, I have her doing nails. Want to give her a try?"

"Nobody trusts her?" Maile asked.

"She's a little young, but she's been through school." Binh barked at the girl who was just finishing with a nail customer. When she came over, Maile could tell she was still a teenager, another Vietnamese girl named Eustice. She looked afraid of her own shadow as Binh gave a verbal resume of Eustice's experience.

Maile handed over the picture. "This is what I need done."

"It's cute. Not so frumpy," Binh said.

"Why do people keep telling me I look frumpy?"

"Sorry, but maybe you do a little." Binh translated, and then translated back to Maile. "She said your hair is pretty and wants to know why you want to cut it off?"

"Tired of being so drab. Can she do that?"

"Be good, okay," Eustice said, after hearing the translation from Binh.

Binh pulled Maile to the empty chair. "Of course she can! Eustice might be young, but she's good."

Binh abandoned Maile and the teenaged stylist when a nail customer appointment arrived.

She watched as the girl combed out her hair in slow motion. It was odd for Maile having someone else other than her mother cut her hair. Just having a non-Hawaiian do that broke a few cultural norms, but those had been flying out the window left and right in her life lately. Maybe the oddest thing would be to have short hair for the first time in her life. When she saw all three feet of it combed out, she started to worry about her idea of updating her hairstyle. It wasn't until she saw the teenager collect a pair of scissors that Maile began to panic. She needed to find a way of stalling to collect her nerves again, but Eustice interrupted her thoughts with a message in Vietnamese.

Binh translated from where she was at the nearby nail station. "Eustice wants to know if you're nervous?"

"Not as much as I thought I'd be, no."

Eustice had something else to say, which prompted embarrassed laughter from everyone in the salon, except Maile. "Eustice wants you to know that she is."

"That's not very reassuring," Maile said, looking at the scissors in the girl's small hand. "I was thinking I could donate it to the wig makers. You know the ones that make wigs for people with cancer?"

After Binh translated, Eustice almost looked relieved at the suggestion, that she was getting time to delay also. When the time came to start the haircut, Binh came to supervise the teenager.

"Maile, maybe you should close your eyes?" Binh said.

"I'm okay."

"I wouldn't be."

"Eustice looks ready to freak out."

"You might be her first real customer."

"Might be?" Maile asked as the pair of scissors came close.

"Definitely the first. So, you have to hold real still, okay? Because I don't know what to expect."

"Now you tell me."

Maile barely breathed as locks of hair were snipped off at shoulder length and set aside. Not quite sure what she thought once the deed was done, if the girl was going to be able to replicate what Maile wanted, or if chaos was ruling the day, she followed her to the shampoo sink. Once she was washed and returned to the chair, she noticed the stylist next to them had started on a new client. She was getting a dye job of some sort, Maile unable to determine the end color. When that client was sent to sit in a chair to wait for the chemicals to do their magic, another client was brought to the chair. While they discussed what was to be done, Maile checked in the mirror for the progress with her own style.

"Eustice, how long have you worked here?" Maile asked, hoping to get a little gossip.

"Yes!"

It was going to be very little gossip. "Okay, good."

The girl in the chair next to her caught Maile's attention. "You'll have to rely on Binh for translation around here. You don't speak any Vietnamese?"

"Just one word," Maile said.

"What's that?"

"Pho."

"Good word to know. You look Hawaiian. How did you end up in a Vietnamese place?"

"Not quite sure right now. Binh and I are old friends."

Binh took over the explanation in Vietnamese, and Maile heard her name mentioned a couple of times. She spent more time watching the other girl get the haircut Maile was hoping for, but at lightning-fast speed from a real stylist.

"Oh, you're that lady?" the other girl asked Maile.

"I am?"

"The one that saved her life that time at the zoo?"

"Oh, that. I didn't do much, but Binh makes it sound like more."

The rest of the women started chatting, while Maile sat still, watching as Eustice struggled with the comb and scissors. Just as the other girl was being finished up with her cut, Binh came over for an inspection. Maile interrupted the browbeating Binh was giving Eustice.

"You see that other girl's hair?" Maile asked them. "That's what I want, if it's not too late."

Binh took Eustice close to the other girl for an inspection of her new style before going back to Maile.

"That's what you want?" Binh asked. "Eustice has been doing something else."

"I don't know what she's been doing, but it doesn't look like that other girl's hair."

Eustice nodded her head almost continuously while Binh gave her a new browbeating. It took another hour for Eustice to finish. When Maile got a closer look in the mirror, she had a hard time recognizing herself, even though the young stylist had somehow recreated something similar to what been done with the other client earlier.

"You really do look good, not so frumpy now," Binh said.

"Yeah, thanks. I never knew being fashionable could be so frightening," Maile said, trying to pay.

"No need to pay. For all the deals we've made, and for how you saved my life that time, I figure I'm way ahead."

Waiting at the bus stop, Maile tugged at the little bit of hair that showed from beneath her hat. When she got to Waikiki, she made the rounds to as many hotel lobbies as she could, leaving brochures for her tour company in racks. She even had the chance to hand out a few business cards to people she met, hoping to get their business. As it was, Susan was already getting some repeat business, mostly with Japanese tourists and American kids that liked her energy. Her tour business was going well; all she could do was hope it continued.

But that afternoon, she had bigger ideas in her mind, and they all concerned Brock.

Waikiki Beach was probably the most famous of all Hawaiian tourist locations, even more than Diamond Head, Pearl Harbor, or Ala Moana Mall. Not much more than a quarter mile long, other beaches bookended it on either side, something many people did not realize. Otherwise, it was narrow through most of it, and spots in the shade of palms was at a premium, especially in the mid-afternoon. Kids hung out at several surfboard rental stands, and highly photographed lifeguard stations were positioned close together. When she got to Duke Kahanamoku's statue near the sidewalk, she followed the walkway to the beach. That was where she and Brock planned to meet that afternoon.

Maile had come prepared. She took a beach towel from her bag and spread it out in a quiet spot near where she hoped a palm tree would bring shade in a few more minutes. Pulling off her blouse and shorts, she was already dressed in a bikini she'd had since her college days but rarely wore.

"I don't remember this being so tight," she whispered to herself, as she stretched out on her towel.

It was too bright to use her phone, so after tucking that away, she set about people watching. Visitors from far and wide littered the beach, wearing every conceivable outfit or style of swimsuit imaginable. She realized she was seeing the place for the last time, at least for a few years. A subtle sense of poignancy slipped into her heart then, letting her know her hours at home were counting down. She would be returning to her real career as a nurse within a few days, the easy days of being a tour guide having slipped away. She still couldn't believe she owned a company, with real employees, something that was earning her money. She also had a boyfriend, something else that was new, and someone she'd have to say goodbye to. She wasn't sure how heartbreaking that moment would be when it came, but was prepared for whatever her heart and soul brought to her.

When sweat began to run, she put on her hat and sunglasses, and wiped down with a towel. By the time she was done wiping and had a drink of water, she was in a full sweat again. It was as much as she had perspired during the marathon run a few weeks earlier, something her mind had forgotten about as quickly as her body. In all ways, she'd moved on from that endurance test, having proven to herself she could do it.

Maile thought of the other endurance tests she'd suffered lately, of long days with difficult tour clients, being held captive in the Royal Palace by gunmen, long counseling sessions with Reverend Ka'uhane and her mother, trips to the women's cellblock at the police station, and even the marathon haircut she'd got a couple hours before. From only a year before, everything had been turned topsy-turvy in her life, but somehow she'd managed to remain upright.

When she spotted Brock coming down the beach scanning back and forth looking for someone, for her, she simply watched until he drew close enough for her to talk to him. She decided to play a game with him, which required disguising her voice with a lower pitch than usual.

"Looking for a good time, sailor?" she said, when he got to within a few steps of her feet.

"No, thanks."

"I don't look fun enough for you?"

He barely glanced at her. "Sorry, I'm looking for someone."

"Wahine?"

"Yep."

"Hoa wahine?"

Brock was scanning the water now. "Sure is."

"O kau wahine?" she asked.

"Not yet."

"Maybe you should ask her to be?"

He finally turned around to look down at her. "Why is it any of your business?"

"You look okay to me. I'd marry you." Maile shifted a little on the beach blanket. She decided to go easy on him and took off her hat and sunglasses, and smiled. "Are you going to ask me or not?"

"Maile?"

"Still think I'm frumpy looking?" She scooted over on the towel to make room for him next to her.

He gently kissed her. "What happened to your hair?"

"Eustice happened to it."

"I don't understand."

She ran her fingers through her hair, still surprised at the length. "It wasn't supposed to be this short."

"Did something go wrong?" he asked.

"Everything was going great, until Eustice got out her scissors. One thing led to another, until I realized something got lost in the translation, and now I look like my Aunt Kelani. You don't like it?"

"You look fantastic. But why the sudden change?"

"Not so sudden. I've known it was coming for several weeks."

"Does it have something to do with your new job?"

"Yeah, I guess the time has come." Maile turned up on her side to face him. Her hand found his and held it tightly. "You're looking at the newest recruit to the United States Army Nurse Corps."

"You've joined the Army?"

"Surprise!"

"Wow. I never expected that. I think people have been figuring you got a crappy job somewhere and were too embarrassed to talk about it. That's the big secret you're been holding all this time?"

"Yep. That's where I'm going tomorrow. I'll have a few weeks of basic training, then learn how to be an officer, and then learn how the military runs its hospitals and how to function as a military nurse. It'll be months before I know where I'll be working."

"With any luck, you'll be assigned to Tripler Medical Center here on Oahu."

"Honestly, I'd like to see a few other places. I'll be back here soon enough."

"Well, the military is good at doing that. Just so you know, you don't get much choice in where you're assigned. When you get your assignment, you just pack your bags and go."

"One less decision I have to make, which is fine with me." She gave him a playful pinch. "That was a dirty trick you played on me back at the police station."

"Hundred percent Ota's doing. It was pretty funny, though. You should've seen your face when that officer put the cuff on you. Talk about pissed."

"Don't ever do that to me again, understand?"

"Is this my first lesson in being obedient to you?"

"You know it. Speaking of decisions..." Maile rummaged through her bag for something hidden at the bottom. She handed him the small box. "...I have this for you. It's a late Christmas gift. I was planning to give it to you that day, but you were too busy yawning, with your eyes at half-mast. At this point, it's more of a going away gift."

He took the box and rattled it. "What is it?"

"Hopefully, not broken. Open it."

He pulled away the small ribbon and popped open the top. "A ring?"

"You don't like it?"

"I like it fine."

"Too soon?"

"I don't know what it means."

"It means I'm coming back to you." She couldn't help but notice he wasn't putting it on. "If you want me to?"

"Yeah, about that." He reached into his pocket for a box of his own and handed it to her. "You beat me to it."

Maile didn't wait to open her box. She'd never had a real ring except for the wedding ring from Robbie, which was promptly sold upon their separation, even before they were divorced. The gold was a deep yellow, and the arrangement of sparkly stones around a larger center stone nearly glowed in the sunlight.

"Does this mean the same as mine?" she asked.

"I think so."

"Think we should wear them?"

"I think we should wear them when you come back here. You know, in an official way."

"I think that's a good idea. Wait until we have more time together," she said.

Maile took the ring from the box and slipped it onto her finger.

"I thought we were waiting?" he asked.

"You do what you want. I'm wearing mine until tomorrow morning."

"You're taking it with you?" he asked.

"I'm putting it in a safe place where it'll be protected day and night?"

"Safe deposit box?

"With my mom. She'll take care of it." She wanted to add one or two kahuna spells would likely be put on it. She watched as the sunlight flashed through the diamond. “Pretty.”

“That center stone is a Princess cut, and the smaller stars around it represent…”

“I know. The Princess cut because I’m one, and the stars for ala waiu, right?”

“I was thinking of your name,” he said. “What’s ala waiu?”

“Milky Way Galaxy. Brah, brush up on your Hawaiian language skills. I can’t teach our kids all by myself.”

“Kids? Isn’t that thinking ahead a little?”

“Brah, my mother had names picked out for our kids when we were still kids.”

“We’ve only been together for a month and we’re already planning kids. Anything else I need to know?” he asked.

“Yeah. Four years and nine months from today, plan on sitting in a delivery room holding your first-born.” Maile kissed him. “I have a question for you.”

Brock lay on his back. “There’s nothing between me and Miss Wong, never was.”

Maile laughed. “That’s good to know. What I’m curious about is what’s the deal with Lopaka and Detective Ota? They have a grudge or what?”

“That started before I joined the force. Why?”

“It drives me nuts not knowing,” she said.

“You have to know everything about everybody, don’t you?”

“Yep.” She smiled down at him. “And I’m making a lifetime project out of you.”

***

In the morning, Maile had no hope of seeing Brock before she left the cottage behind for her trip to the airport. There would be no grand gesture of him rushing to the airport just in time to kiss her goodbye, no memory of a romantic Hollywood moment to cling to, no last picture together before she left him to look at during the hard days that were sure to come. All she could do was take the predawn bus to the airport and wait for her flight.

After checking in at her gate, she wandered aimlessly through the gift shops before going to Starbucks for a quick jolt. Leaving the busy shop with her cup, she did a double-take when she saw someone at a table, sipping coffee, looking at her phone. It was her first surprise of the day and the sun hadn't even come up yet. She went to that table for a closer look at the young woman.

"Honey?"

She looked up from her phone. "What're you doing here?"

"Why do people keep asking me that?" Maile said.

"Why wouldn't I?"

"Never mind that. Are you going somewhere?"

"I'm going home."

Maile was as confused now as with everything else related to the Swenbergs, Laurie, and Honey. "You're just coming in from somewhere?"

"Um, hello? This is the departures terminal. That means I'm leaving."

"Don't talk to me like that, please." Maile drew up a chair and sat at the table with Honey. "You're going back to LA?"

"I've had enough trouble, in LA, here, anywhere. If I went to New York, I'd have trouble there."

"Then where are you going?"

"Home to Spain. I can stay at my parents place until I figure out what to do. They have plenty of room, with a little guest house I can live in for a while."

Maile scanned the area around them. "Where's Clarice?"

Honey went back to looking at her phone. "Home."

"She's already gone to Spain?"

"She's at home with the Longs."

"Oh, you're coming back to get her later?" Maile asked.

"What's it to you?"

"Just curious, I guess."

"Quit being my social worker, okay? I don't need your help."

"Not your social worker. It's just seems sad to me that she's not going with you."

Honey put down her phone. "Look, I asked Clarice if she wanted to go to Spain or stay here. She said she wanted to stay here. So I asked again, if she wanted to come with me or stay with the Longs." Honey glared at Maile with wet eyes. "She wanted to stay with them. Happy now that you have your answer?"

"Not really." Maile was heartbroken for Honey, and for Clarice. That's when she noticed Honey had been looking at images of Clarice on her phone, pictures taken while playing at parks, a birthday party at the Long's home, some older baby pictures. When a flight was called to start boarding, she watched as Honey gathered her things. "You're actually going to leave now?"

"Not much choice. I have the ticket. My parents are waiting for me at home in Spain. What I don't have is a life here in Honolulu."

"You have your daughter here. And your friends, the Longs."

"We live in in a house where we're barely tolerated, and they hate me. That old Granny Long is the only one who likes Clarice. Might be better to let her raise her than a misfit like me."

"You're not a misfit. I can tell by the look on your face that leaving Clarice here is breaking your heart. Why not try figuring out something?"

"Like what? I'm no good at any job I ever get. I wasn't even good at being a waitress. I mean, who's so bad at carrying plates of food around that she gets fired? Me, that's who. I don't have a way of supporting her, and she doesn't want to come with me to Spain. That's just the way it goes."

"You grew up speaking Spanish, right? And your English is perfect. Don't you also speak Chinese?"

"I was a terrible student when I was a kid, so my parents got all kinds of tutors for me. Yeah, Chinese was one of them. So?"

"I could really use a trilingual saleswoman and tour guide in my company. I've offered that job to you before. I don't know why you never came in."

"You were sincere?"

"Of course! Are you a citizen of Spain or the US?"

"Oscar got me dual citizenship through a friend he knew in LA." There was another call for Honey's flight, which made her fidget in her chair. "It's legit."

"I'm sure it is." Maile had the ploy of hoping to make Honey miss her flight and have to stay in Honolulu at least for another day or two to reconsider her decision. "You know, I remember your real name is Maria. You must've had a Chinese name before you were adopted."

"Ming Hua. It means bright flower."

"It's a pretty name."

"Chinese names are a lot like Hawaiian names, with a meaning."

"What last name do you go by?"

"Contraves, when I use my Spanish passport. Not Swenberg, that's for sure." Honey didn't seem to notice when the final boarding call was made for her flight. "My real family name is Wu."

"They're the ones who gave you up for adoption. I think your real family is here in Honolulu. What's Clarice's family name?" Maile chanced asking.

"Clarice Contraves Swenberg is on her birth certificate. Not sure I like it, though."

"Maybe you can just stop using Swenberg? Clarice Contraves has a nice sound to it."

Honey looked up from her phone for the first time in several minutes. "It does, doesn't it?"

"She's a sweet little girl." Maile's coffee was finished, but she hoped their conversation wasn't. "You're doing the same thing to her if you leave her behind, that the Wus did to you as a baby."

"Not so easy being a mother," Honey said quietly.

"I've never been one, but from what I've seen, no, it sure isn't."

Over the airport PA system, Honey's name was called. "Will passenger Maria Contraves please report to Gate Nineteen. Maria Contraves, Gate Nineteen, please."

"They're calling for you," Maile said.

"I know. You really think I could do okay at your company?"

"I think if you learned a little more about the famous tourist sites, you'd do great."

"Would they like me? The others at your company?"

Maile knew she had her then. "It's not a very big place, but everybody gets along okay."

After another plea from the airlines for Maria Contraves to board her flight, Honey slowly put away her phone and assembled her things. Maile needed to act, and fast. She got out a couple of business cards from Manoa Tours and jotted something on the back.

"I'm leaving town for a while, but there's a guy named Brian who runs the office. Tell him I sent you in. You'd get paid what I got paid as a guide, which is double minimum wage, and you split your tips with your driver. Plus, you'd get a ten percent sales commission on every paid tour you arrange."

"I can't live with the Longs, and I'm not taking Clarice to a shelter."

Maile jotted an address on the back of the other business card. "This place isn't much, but the rooms are cheap and I happen to know they have a new vacancy. The girl that lives across the hall from the available room is friendly."

Honey took both cards, gave them a quick look, and tucked them away. "Thanks."

Maile watched as Honey left the table. Instead of leaving the airport, she pulled her roll-along suitcase to Gate Nineteen and showed her boarding pass to the gate attendant.

"Don't go," Maile whispered to herself, while watching Honey. "Just turn around."

She watched as Honey went to the door to the jetway, flashed the boarding pass again, and went through, joining the line of passengers at the back. When the door closed behind her, Maile could only shake her head. She checked her phone for the time and any last minute messages, and returned one to her mother. Gathering her things, it was almost time to go to her own gate.

What caught her attention was when the door to Gate Nineteen opened again and someone came out, arguing with the gate attendant about something. Here came Honey, pulling her suitcase behind her. She came straight toward Maile, smiling.

"You really should be a social worker," she said as she went past Maile.

"I'll call the office to let them know someone named Maria is coming in for a job."

Once Maile found her gate, she sat anxiously waiting. It would be the first time she'd even left the shores of Hawaii, and would see new terrain for the first time in her life. It was exciting for her, even if most of the next four years would be spent on military bases and in hospitals. When she heard the first call for her flight, it was time to go. She got her phone, ready to turn it off. Before she could, it rang with a call from Detective Ota.

"Detective, make it fast. I'm standing in line for my flight."

"Yes, the next chapter of your life starts today."

"Is that why you called? To wax philosophical?"

"No. Just one last piece of news."

"You have a serial killer on the loose and you need my help?"

"I hope not. No, this is about your old friend, Prince Aziz."

"For the last time, he's not my friend," she hissed into the phone.

"Well, he made an important friend somewhere, because he's on his way home to Khashraq, free and clear."

"How is that even possible? Never mind. I don't care anymore."

Ota went ahead as if he didn't hear her. "Your other friend, Mrs. Abrams from the Department of Justice had an airtight case against him, but it was someone in the State Department that cut a deal and had him released, on the condition that he and no one in his family ever sets foot on US soil."

"Good for us. And I hope the entire group of them bake in the hot Khashraqi desert where they belong." Something occurred to Maile and she had to ask. "Hey, did anyone ever figure out who stole Ka'uhane's ukulele?"

"Does it matter? He got it back, safe and sound, right?"

"I guess. There's something about that Pete guy, though."

"Maile, do me a favor. You stick to nursing, and let me handle the bad guys in Honolulu, okay?"

With that, she said goodbye to him, almost as glad he was out of her life as Prince Aziz, the Swenbergs, a pair of Brooklynites, and various other misfits that have brought trouble to her beloved Hawaiian nation.

▪ ▪ ▪

More from Kay Hadashi

Maile Spencer Honolulu Tour Guide Mysteries

AWOL at Ala Moana
Baffled at the Beach
Coffee in the Canal
Dead on Diamond Head
Honey of a Hurricane
Malice in the Palace
Keepers of the Kingdom
Peril at the Potluck

The June Kato Intrigue Series

Kimono Suicide
Stalking Silk
Yakuza Lover
Deadly Contact
Orchids and Ice
Broken Protocol

The Island Breeze Series

Island Breeze
Honolulu Hostage
Maui Time
Big Island Business
Adrift
Molokai Madness
Ghost of a Chance

The Melanie Kato Adventure Series

Away

Faith

Risk

Quest

Mission

Secrets

Future

Kahuna

Directive

Nano

The Maui Mystery Series

A Wave of Murder

A Hole in One Murder

A Moonlit Murder

A Spa Full of Murder

A Down to Earth Murder

A Haunted Murder

A Plan for Murder

A Misfortunate Murder

A Quest for Murder

A Game of Murder

The Honolulu Thriller Series

Interisland Flight

Kama'aina Revenge

Tropical Revenge

Waikiki Threat

Rainforest Rescue

Made in the USA
Monee, IL
12 June 2021